PENGUIN CLASSICS

THE PRINCESSE DE CLÈVES

MARIE-MADELEINE PIOCHE DE LA VERGNE was born in Paris in 1634. In 1656 she married the Comte de Lafayette, had two sons and lived on his country estate until 1659. She then returned to Paris and the couple remained largely separate from then on. She started a literary *salon* with her close friends Madame de Sévigné and the Duc de La Rochefoucauld, who was a major influence on her intellectual development. She also mixed in court circles and wrote a biography of her friend Henriette, wife of the Duc d'Orléans, after the princess's early death in 1670. Her posthumously published memoirs of the court are useful for historians, but she is remembered chiefly for her novels which, unlike the interminable romances of her predecessors, are characterized by a search for proportion and an overriding interest in psychology. Apart from her masterpiece, *La Princesse de Clèves*, she wrote *La Princesse de Montpensier*, *Zaïde* and *La Comtesse de Tende*. Madame de Lafayette died in 1693.

Robin Buss is a lecturer, writer and translator who works as film critic for the *Independent on Sunday* and television critic for *The Times Educational Supplement*. He studied at the University of Paris, where he took a degree and a doctorate in French literature. He is part-author of the article 'French Literature' in *Encyclopaedia Britannica* and has published critical studies of works by Vigny and Cocteau and two books on European cinema, *The French Through Their Films* (1988) and *Italian Films* (1989). He has also edited Stendhal's *Lucien Leuwen* and translated *Letters from Russia* by the Marquis de Custine for Penguin Classics.

The Princesse de Clèves

MME DE LAFAYETTE

TRANSLATED
WITH AN INTRODUCTION AND NOTES BY
ROBIN BUSS

PENGUIN BOOKS

PENGUIN BOOKS

Published by the Penguin Group
27 Wrights Lane, London W8 5TZ, England
Penguin Books USA Inc., 40 West 23rd Street, New York, New York 10010, USA
Penguin Books Australia Ltd, Ringwood, Victoria, Australia
Penguin Books Canada Ltd, 10 Alcorn Avenue, Toronto, Ontario, Canada, M4V 3B2
Penguin Books (NZ) Ltd, 182–190 Wairau Road, Auckland 10, New Zealand

Penguin Books Ltd, Registered Offices: Harmondsworth, Middlesex, England

La Princesse de Clèves
first published 1678
Published in Penguin Books 1962
Reprinted in Penguin Classics 1978
This translation, Introduction and Notes published in Penguin Classics 1992

Introduction, translation and Notes copyright © Robin Buss, 1992
All rights reserved

The moral right of the translator has been asserted

Filmset in Monophoto 10½/12 Monophoto Garamond
Printed in England by Clays Ltd, St Ives plc

Contents

Introduction

———

Before the end of the year 1678, in which *The Princesse de
Clèves* was published, the novel was subjected to rigorous
analysis in a *Letter to the Marquise de *** on the 'Princesse
de Clèves'*. The author, Valincour, criticized the book's use
of language, the behaviour of the characters and the plausibility of the plot. But even he succumbed to its charm: 'I
admit that I cannot remember reading anything so vivid and
touching in my life.' And, from Valincour onwards, a story
that Stendhal pronounced 'divine' and the first novel in
French, as much for its intrinsic worth as by reason of its
date, has continued to disarm critics and to delight its
readers.

Conventional histories of literature agree with Stendhal's
judgement of this as the prototype of the modern novel in
French.

There are vestiges of traditional story-telling devices ... but they
are intended to work in relation to the central story rather than as
ends in themselves ... And, even if it lacks realistic detail and local
colour, this one text, by its basic credibility, depth of character
analysis and capacity to embrace serious moral issues, marks the
start of the novel's evolution into the major genre into which, in
later centuries, it will develop.*

More specifically, *The Princesse de Clèves* is sometimes considered to have set the agenda for a peculiarly French

———

*Colin Radford, Christopher Shorley, Mary Hossain, *Signposts to French
Literature* (London, Hutchinson, 1988).

contribution to the European novel: an overriding concern with psychological analysis, a certain 'purity' of language and classical simplicity of plot. The first of these led Kléber Haedens to see it as a 'preliminary sketch' for Proust, at the very least in its concept of love as inseparable from anguish. We can also see debts to the novel in Raymond Radiguet's *Le Bal du comte d'Orgel*, in Françoise Sagan's *Bonjour tristesse*, and in Cocteau, who wrote the screenplay for Jean Delannoy's film adaptation of the novel. Its place on the syllabus is firmly established and its qualities are so immediately appealing that it might seem the least problematic of all literary classics in French.

Apart, that is, from the question of authorship. *The Princesse de Clèves* was published anonymously and Mme de Lafayette publicly denied any claim to the work. It is now generally accepted that the book is hers, and that her friends La Rochefoucauld and Segrais contributed, at most, minor corrections. There is also the matter of origins: not so much the sources for the historical part of the novel, which is set roughly a century before it was written, as the extent to which Mme de Lafayette drew on her knowledge of court life in her own time and intended the story to be read as a kind of allegory, or even a *roman-à-clef*. But the specificity of the historical details suggests otherwise. If the court of Henri II is used as a figure for anything, it is to serve as an enclosed, at times claustrophobic stage for the action, where the actors are prisoners of their privileged status: from the first meeting, Mme de Clèves is forced into intimacy with the Duc de Nemours and her attempts to escape her dilemma through flight are repeatedly thwarted by the obligations of court life. So what we have is an imagined love story, given authenticity by its author's experience of aristocratic society and by conscientious research into the historical events against which it is set. Why suspect anything more devious than that?

Nothing devious, then, or esoteric, but the contrary: a story that is moving precisely because it is simple. Yet, the more one considers the meanings of the text, the more intriguing it seems. The structure, the characters, the treatment of love, politics and, above all, of serious moral issues, appear full of ambivalence. There is an intellectual framework behind the touching emotions and presumed moral values, which is puzzlingly at odds with them. *The Princesse de Clèves* is a romance against love, with a hero who is an anti-hero and a heroine who is a victim of circumstance, whose life is destroyed by passion, and yet who convinces us throughout that she retains control of her fate. The plot and the language are so direct that they become opaque and invite questions, both about the nature of passion and about the nature of power. Even the opening words of praise for the splendour of Henri II's court turn out to be more than just a conventional device for setting the scene, which is how we are likely to read them at first.

On that first reading, the beginning of *The Princesse de Clèves* is tedious, and particularly frustrating in a translation. Not only do we have to contend with those details of the sixteenth-century French nobility, given as a bewildering list of personalities and factions (it is a relief to come across the familiar figure of Mary Stuart); but the information is presented in terms that seem designed to make us doubt their authority. Henri II's court, we are asked to believe, was unsurpassed in splendour and magnificence, inhabited by the most handsome men and the most beautiful women that ever lived. This does not even have the merit of a history lesson, and we soon suspect that the author is exaggerating the attractions of her historical setting as a means to enhance the appeal of the story.

We are right to think that she has some design on us in the use of all these superlatives, but quite wrong if we imagine that they are just for purposes of advertising. The idea of a golden age, a privileged moment in historical time, plays an important role in the novel. It is not introduced either for nationalistic reasons, to promote an image of a glorious past, or for hedonistic ones, to induce a sense of well-being. The last years of Henri II's reign are described in these opening pages as improbably fine, but only in contrast to the civil unrest that followed – and not by accident: this court of beautiful people is the site of bitter conflicts, and all its inhabitants, as we gradually discover, are destined for tragic fates. In short, as Mme de Chartres tells her daughter, the heroine of the novel, 'if you judge by appearances in this place ... you will often be deceived, because what appears to be the case hardly ever is.'

What is true of the court is true of the novel. The historical background is neither purely decorative, nor a history lesson, but a morality, giving a social and political dimension to the story of Mme de Clèves and her love for the Duc de Nemours. At a symbolic level, the love between the princess and the duke is reflected in the history of their time.

Having said that, the lasting appeal of their story depends on something else that, at first sight, may not appear to be the case: *The Princesse de Clèves* is a story of erotic love. So deceptive is its eroticism that the statement could seem ridiculous, especially to modern readers. After all, the two central characters in this love story never so much as touch hands; in fact, we are told that the first time they even meet each other alone is also the last. The author is mistaken about this, because she has forgotten the episode of the letter earlier in the book, but the detail is academic. Surely it is straining the meaning of the term to call the emotions that the author describes 'erotic'?

One answer to that depends on a reading of the text that would not have occurred to Mme de Lafayette or her contemporaries. The Princesse de Clèves and the Duc de Nemours fall in love at first sight, and from that moment the sense of sight becomes the channel and the figure for their desire. Take the scene where the duke observes Mme de Clèves from the garden of her husband's country house at Coulommiers. The circumstances are of the kind that Valincour rightly criticized as far-fetched: spied on (indirectly) by her husband, Nemours has made his way into the garden and observes her in a pavilion, or sort of summerhouse, where she is binding up a malacca cane that once belonged to him. She then turns away from this to gaze at a painting that happens to include his portrait.

While she looks at his image, he looks at her. Unaware that she is being observed, she is sitting on a divan, casually dressed, with nothing around her head or shoulders but her hair, loosely tied.

> He saw that she was alone, but saw such astonishing beauty in her that he was scarcely able to contain himself at the sight . . . To see – in the depth of night, in the loveliest spot in the world – to see the person whom he adored, to see her without her knowing that she was seen, and to see her entirely occupied with matters relating to himself . . . is something no other lover has ever enjoyed or imagined.

The conclusion – in the literal sense absurd, since no one can deny that other lovers have imagined and enjoyed intenser pleasures than this – merely serves to underline what is really going on. The writing may be constrained by literary convention, but this does not prevent Mme de Lafayette from evoking the intimacy of the encounter and the vulnerability of the heroine, who unconsciously offers herself to Nemours with her hair casually tied and her throat uncovered; or from the obsessive repetition of the verb 'to see'. The duke remains 'motionless' and the pair are transported outside time in an act of what could be described as mutual voyeurism.

But to make the sexual nature of the encounter explicit is to put an unnecessary gloss on it: the emotions, and the nature of the emotions, are all there in the text. The problem we may have in discerning them, on a superficial reading of the novel, is partly to do with literary and social conventions, and with the language in which they are expressed. Mme de Lafayette, in the passage I have just quoted, and throughout the book, uses the word *amant* of her two main protagonists; today, this means 'lover' and, as in English, implies a sexual relationship.

However, in seventeenth-century French, the word was both more specific and less: a standard modern dictionary of classical French (the Larousse *Dictionnaire du français classique*, 1988) defines a 'lover' as any man who *declares* his love to a woman, regardless of whether or not he may be sincere; and this emphasis on the act of speech, with none on the act of sex, entirely displaces the relationship from the private to the social sphere, where it acquires an element of play. Love is not just a matter of inclination, but part of a social game in which the expression of feeling may be a move as crucial as physical intimacy and where, as a result, everything depends on the degree of sincerity behind what is said.

This is why Mme de Clèves, forced into daily contact with him by her obligations as a member of the court, makes such strenuous efforts to avoid any situation in which Nemours can cross this barrier and declare what he feels (or may be pretending to feel); why, too, the characters attach such importance to honesty in the statement of feeling, which is also one of the themes around which the whole story revolves. The sincerity of the players clearly decides the course of the game.

Yet not altogether in the way that one might expect: M. de Clèves claims to attach great moral importance to sincerity, and tells his wife a cautionary tale to illustrate the fact, but when it comes to the point, he finds himself unable to abide by his principles. The word 'lover' may be used indiscriminately for any participant in the courtly game of love, regardless of whether his feelings are real or feigned, but this does not mean that the reality of the feelings is unimportant. On the contrary, for the book's original readers as much as for us, what makes Mme de Clèves and the Duc de Nemours 'lovers' is also the nature of the feeling they arouse in one another and its difference in kind from other varieties of love.

Irrational, instantaneous, inspired by the mere sight of its object, this passionate love is in essence uncontrollable, threatening and, consequently, subversive of the very idea of the social ritual that is played out in its name. This is the destructive emotion that implants itself in M. de Clèves when he first sees his wife, and it can only be satisfied by evidence of a corresponding feeling in her. And, clearly, this love is not mere affection, respect, esteem, or indeed any reasoned or even primarily altruistic feeling, but an erotic passion, regardless of whether we interpret this as meaning sexual desire, romantic love or the interference of a playful and ill-mannered god in the course of human affairs.

Men and women are equally subject to this passion, which is the motive force of the novel, but suffer unequally from the effects. The only happiness for a woman, Mme de Chartres tells her daughter, the heroine of the book, is to love her husband and to be loved by him; and we accept the statement, at first reading, at face value, assuming that it reflects the author's point of view as well as a conventional one. But in that case, why does Mme de Chartres knowingly allow her daughter to marry a man whom she does not love? The ostensible motive is social advancement: the Prince de Clèves is a good match and Mme de Chartres's other plans have fallen through. Does she then sacrifice her daughter to ambition? And what are we to make of her distress when she realizes that Mme de Clèves is falling in love with the Duc de Nemours?

Again, on the face of it, there is no reason why Mme de Clèves should not enjoy the happiness that comes from loving her husband, who does love her. They are well-matched, in social status and age. We may have the impression that he is older than the Duc de Nemours, and perhaps this is deliberate: M. de Clèves, we are told, has a prudence 'hardly ever found in young men' and his wife's willingness to confide in him suggests that she sees him as a father-figure. Yet the difference between him and Nemours is not one of age, but the Prince de Clèves's exceptional ability to remain loyal in love, contrasted with the Duc de Nemours's exceptional ability to inspire it. The princess is caught in a tragic dilemma, offered the possibility of happiness with a loving husband, but driven to reject it by an impulse more powerful than the desire for happiness.

'I may be led by passion,' she says, 'but it cannot blind me.' It does not blind her to the faults of the Duc de Nemours or to the likelihood that she would not ultimately find lasting happiness with a man who is almost irresistible to other women, as much as to herself. She has discovered that she is the same as these others in her capacity for falling in love, and different from them in her ability to withstand his advances. Men and women share the same passion but are different in their capacity to sustain it, the novel implies, either because of some innate difference, or because of the roles that marriage and society impose on them. For the heroine of the book, renunciation – and a form of death, if not death itself – may be the only path that allows her to keep control of her fate.

And when he falls on his knees, she replies, *smiling*, that what she has told him, he knows only too well. With that smile, bought at the price of a terrible lucidity, the victim triumphs, over the man who is pursuing her, over her own misery, over her social role, over her fate. But the triumph is in no way consoling: this novel, motivated by the power of passionate love, is not in either the usual or the literary sense, a romantic novel, but quite simply anti-romantic, refusing to believe that passion can bring anything but pain, even in a romance, and creating a powerful tension out of this conflict between its simultaneous acknowledgement and rejection of erotic love. Nor is this conclusion based on conventional Christian morality, but on a view of human nature that is largely uninformed by notions of right and wrong.

'Man is a reed,' the Duc de La Rochefoucauld wrote, '. . . but a thinking reed'; in other words, bent by passion, without being blinded by it. Not surprisingly, in view of his friendship with Mme de Lafayette, La Rochefoucauld has been suggested as a possible contributor to *The Princesse de Clèves*. But it is far more likely that these characters were created by Mme de Lafayette alone, which makes one curious about her; because, as she remarks in relation to the Duc de Nemours, it is a fairly common indiscretion 'to speak in general terms of one's particular feelings and to describe one's own adventures under assumed names'.

Mme de Lafayette was born Marie-Madeleine de la Vergne, in March 1634, the eldest daughter of Marc Pioche de la Vergne and Isabelle Péna (herself daughter of the king's physician). Her parents, who had two other daughters, were comfortably off; her father, a mathematician and scientist, held various government posts and was able to have a house built at the corner of the Rue de Vaugirard and the Rue Férou, which Marie-Madeleine was to inhabit for most of her life. But he died when she was only fifteen, and in 1650 her mother married René-Renaud de Sévigné, a family friend who appears to have been considered originally as a husband for Marie-Madeleine. Through this lost husband, she found a friend: René-Renaud was the uncle by marriage of Marie de Rabutin-Chantal, Marquise de Sévigné, whose correspondence (though not published until the following century) was to make her the most celebrated letter-writer in European literature.

Roger Duchêne, in a recent biography (*Madame de La Fayette*, Paris, 1988), says that Marie-Madeleine was profoundly affected by the disappointment of her mother's remarriage: 'Never again would she trust anyone blindly ... She was determined never again to depend on anyone. She would be strong ...' For the moment, the arrival of this step-father considerably influenced the course of her life. It meant that she had to look elsewhere for a husband. Secondly, it gave her an entirely unsentimental attitude to her father's inheritance: her mother had not been able to deprive the children of their rights, but made over to her husband one quarter of Marc Pioche's estate, the maximum she was legally entitled to dispose of in this way. As for Marie-Madeleine, she seems to have had no regrets when her two younger sisters decided to take religious vows and enter a convent. As nuns, they renounced all of their inheritance except a small annuity. Marie-Madeleine thus became heir to a substantial fortune.

René-Renaud also introduced her, indirectly, to a world of political intrigue. He had been implicated in the movements known as the Fronde, inspired by opposition to Louis XIV's powerful but unpopular minister Mazarin. René-Renaud and the Sévignés were allied to Mazarin's leading opponent, François de Gondi, Cardinal de Retz; and Marie-Madeleine would certainly have recalled these factional struggles of her own day when she came to describe those at the court of Henri II, in *The Princesse de Clèves*.

Finally, René-Renaud contributed significantly to her education. In 1651, he introduced her to the poet and scholar Gilles Ménage, already a friend of Mme de Sévigné, who was to become Marie-Madeleine's tutor, confidant, 'lover' (at least, in the wide connotations of the time), and the most important influence in her intellectual development. A leading figure in literary circles who had just published an etymological dictionary of the French language, he has the reputation of a pedant, due partly to his caricature as 'Vadius' in Molière's play *Les Femmes savantes*. In his poetry, he addressed Marie-Madeleine as 'Laverna'. He was thirty-six, she was seventeen. She would tease him by refusing to conjugate the Latin verb *amare*, 'to love', in any tense except the future.

There seems little doubt that it was not conjugated in the present when, four years later, she married Jean-François Motier, Comte de Lafayette, eighteen years her senior. Marriage gave her a name, security and two sons. It also took her away from Paris, to her husband's property in Auvergne. For the first six years, the couple stayed alternately in the country and in Paris, returning to the capital to settle affairs after the death of her mother, then back to Auvergne, where Jean-François was engaged in a prolonged dispute over his own estates. In 1658, she went to the spa at Vichy for her health, which had been troubling her since her mother's remarriage. Finally, in 1661, her husband returned alone to his country home.

Perhaps it is unfair to present him, as Nancy Mitford did in the preface to her translation of *The Princesse de Clèves* (Penguin, Harmondsworth, 1950), as merely a bore to whom Marie-Madeleine had to do her duty by producing children (two sons and at least one child stillborn), before she could persuade him that the country disagreed with her health. The two appear to have understood one another and to have fulfilled what were probably equally modest expectations from the marriage. The closeness of his relationship with Abbé Bayard leads Duchêne to hint that he may have been bisexual. She, on reaching her legal majority at twenty-five, acquired some freedom to manage her own financial affairs. Even before that, he had taken the exceptional step of giving her equal rights in the disposal of her possessions (though marriage had made her legally a 'minor' and subject entirely to him). Now, with her husband almost permanently absent, she was also free to pursue her social ambitions, as a wife whose status had been improved by alliance with her husband's family.

Her literary ambition is less distinct and was probably less important: it would contribute nothing to her standing in society to be recognized as the author of novels, which is why she always publicly denied authorship of the greatest among her works. During her absence in Auvergne, Ménage and Mme de Sévigné kept her in touch with political and intellectual life, particularly the literature of 'preciosity'. The *précieuses*, satirized by Molière in *Les Précieuses ridicules*, sought to refine the arts of writing and conversation, and cultivated an extreme form of platonic love, analysing and classifying every stage and shade of feeling to produce the novelist Mlle de Scudéry's allegorical Carte de Tendre, a map describing the progress of the affections, from First Acquaintance, towards the three cities of Tendre on their respective rivers of Esteem, Gratitude and Inclination, via Sincerity, Attentiveness and so on, the traveller hoping to avoid the paths that will lead to the Lake of Indifference or the Sea of Hostility. Ménage sent Marie-Madeleine the latest parts of

Mlle de Scudéry's *Clélie*, a ten-volume romance set in ancient Rome (and published between 1654 and 1660) in which the Carte de Tendre appeared.

It is wrong to see the *précieuses* simply as they were caricatured by Molière. Their concern for language was salutary, and their attitude to love seems a valid response at a time when women could enjoy considerable influence, but almost solely through men rather than in their own right. The *précieuse* approached sexual relationships with a mixture of prudishness and coquetry, thus retaining the largest possible space in which to exercise power. A minute analysis of the psychology of love was a necessary science for her and its description in such apparently frivolous conceits as the Carte de Tendre, the means of establishing a set of rules for social behaviour of which she thus became the acknowledged legislator. There is nothing ridiculous about such ingenuity, except when it is judged by the standards of those who have no need to employ it.

After Mme de Lafayette settled in Paris in 1658, on her return from Vichy, her salon was a meeting-place for the *précieuses* and from 1661 she herself became the close confidante of Henrietta of England, daughter of Charles I and Henrietta Maria, and wife of the King's brother, Philippe d'Orléans. Henrietta was ten years younger than Marie-Madeleine (who wrote a life of the princess, after her tragically early death in 1770): the friendship is a clear model for that between the heroine and Mary Stuart, the Dauphine, in *The Princesse de Clèves*. At this time, Mme de Lafayette also made her literary début. Her first novel, *La Princesse de Montpensier*, appeared anonymously in 1662, and was attributed to Ménage. Her second, *Zaÿde*, was published in 1669 under the name of Jean de Segrais, with a preface by Pierre-Daniel Huet, which set out to give the Novel greater respectability as a genre, by tracing its origins back to classical epic poetry.

Segrais was one of those who had started to take over the place previously occupied by Ménage, but he was by no means the most significant. From now on, the most important masculine influence in her life was François, Duc de La Rochefoucauld (1613–80), another former participant in the Fronde against Mazarin, who is remembered as the author of a collection of maxims giving succinct and often cynical analyses of human behaviour. As with her other mentors, the precise nature of her relationship with La Rochefoucauld is unclear, though it was hinted that they were lovers.

Certainly, the friendship with La Rochefoucauld caused a breach with Ménage, not healed for many years. Even Mme de Sévigné acknowledged that there was a certain coldness in Mme de Lafayette's character; there was at least an absence of sentimentality that had made her welcome the sacrifice of her sisters to religion for the sake of their inheritance, and ensured from then on that she never ceased to calculate her own best interests. Yet she retained the loyalty of many friends, most of all Mme de Sévigné, with whom she was capable of laughter and real affection. 'You are the person whom I have most truly loved,' she wrote at the end of her life. She was constantly subject to ill-health and, understandably, at times to depression. Perhaps the coldness is easily explained by early disappointments: her father's death, her mother's remarriage (to the man intended for herself) and the relative failure of her own marriage to M. de Lafayette. Perhaps it could even be seen as indicating her maturity and intelligence (Boileau described her as the woman who had most wit and wrote best of any in France), her refusal to be carried away by emotion, and her skill in the management of affairs. Through her social position, her financial independence, her literary salon and her relations with the court, she possessed exceptional influence and power for a woman of her time. But she was too clever not to realize how fragile and limited it was, even so. The complexities of her character, her capacity for feeling and the lucidity of her mind are all evident in *The Princesse de Clèves*.

The novel appeared in March 1678 and was promoted,

especially through the periodical *Le Mercure galant*, with what Roger Duchêne describes as the first campaign of its kind in the history of publishing. It was an immediate success: the first English translation of 'the most famed romance written in French by the greatest Wits of France' dates from 1679.

With the exception of *Zaïde*, which is Mme de Lafayette's attempt at a conventional romance, her novels suggest comparisons with drama rather than with earlier prose fiction. The characters, moral universe, 'unity of action' and, above all, the language of *The Princesse de Clèves* belong recognizably to the same cultural milieu as the tragedies of Racine and Corneille. Mme de Lafayette's vocabulary, though larger than the austere dictionary of Racine, similarly loads certain key terms with exceptional weight of significance: *passion, inclination, galanterie, honnêteté, attachement, amant, péril*. Even when such words have not changed perceptibly in meaning since the seventeenth century (as *amant* has, for example), they acquire peculiar connotations by the frequency of their use in the novel. The modern French reader needs to treat them with care and they offer special problems to a translator.

This inhibited language and the uncomplicated plot give *The Princesse de Clèves* an appearance of clarity and simplicity that is not deceptive, since it directs us to the idea that a single word, like *honnêteté*, necessarily implies a complex of social meanings, and *passion*, a chaos of emotions. The words most charged with significance in the novel's description of its characters' feelings are the simple terms *trouble* and *inquiétude*, which recur over and over, to convey the turmoil and anguish of passion, with different overtones according to whether the reaction is inspired by desire, jealousy, uncertainty or joy. People may (and, in *The Princesse de Clèves*, do) die for love – or renounce it for what is contained in the word *repos* (which consequently implies something more profound than merely 'rest' or 'peace and quiet').

If the words are plain signs for complex realities, so is the novel. In terms of the narrative, an extension outwards from the particular towards a wider significance is suggested by the interpolated episodes: Mme de Chartres's story of the Duchesse de Valentinois (Book One); the stories of Mme de Tournon and Anne Boleyn (Book Two); the story of the Vidame de Chartres (Books Two and Three). Each of these enriches the narrative or the historical background and makes some point about the relationship between men and women: Henri II's fidelity to his mistress, the Duchesse de Valentinois, in contrast to the vulnerability of King Henry VIII's wife, Anne Boleyn; the insincerity and infidelity of both Mme de Tournon and the Vidame de Chartres. No particular moral is stated, but the four stories contribute to an underlying message about the perils of sexual love, while forming part of Mme de Clèves's education in the ways of the society around her and nourishing her reflections – and ours – on her situation.

In terms of the characters, the novel creates a sense of depth by varying the mode of discourse to allow different viewpoints on the action. The feelings of Mme de Clèves, M. de Nemours and M. de Clèves are conveyed through dialogue and monologue, interior monologue or free indirect speech. In M. de Nemours's case, he appears first as he looks to the court: the handsomest among many handsome men, who impresses Mme de Clèves and is captivated by her beauty. In their conversations, he expresses himself in the oblique terms of the gallant lover making flirtatious advances, while observing her reactions (for example, her jealousy over the lost letter) with the cool eye of a man well-practised in the conduct of such affairs.

As the story progresses, we penetrate further into the man. His thoughts and feelings are directly described ('... how agitated he felt! What terror that he might annoy her!') or revealed in interior monologue ('"For she does indeed love me," he said ...'). Even here, as has frequently been remarked, he retains the instincts of a predator, calculating his best move, but the privileged access that the author allows us engages our sympathy by convincing us of the sincerity of his emotions.

Nonetheless, there is a continuity between the duke's public and private personae that distinguishes him from the female characters in the book: the emotions that he pretends in the guise of a conventional lover are the same as those revealed in his most intimate interior monologue, however subject to erosion by time and absence, because convention permits him, as a man, to express his desires through the rituals of courtship. The same is not true, for example, of the Queen, as she reveals in her conversation with the Vidame de Chartres (at the end of Book Two): in appearance, she tells him, she tolerates the King's affair with the Duchesse de Valentinois, but in private it torments her; and it is necessary, especially for those of her rank, to have one person, at least, in whom to confide. The irony is that she is wrong to trust the Vidame, and we only learn that she has taken him into her confidence because he is giving a verbatim account of her remarks to the Duc de Nemours.

'I set . . . great store by sincerity,' M. de Clèves claims to Sancerre, in a conversation he subsequently reports to his wife: there is more here, however, than simply the dramatic irony which Mme de Lafayette points out in the next paragraph ('she saw some reference . . . to her own situation'). Yet the virtues that people proclaim are not always those they expect, or those that are beneficial to individuals or to society. Even as he acknowledges the exceptional honesty of her confession to him, M. de Clèves is tormented by the idea that she might show equal 'sincerity' to Nemours, and let him know his feelings are reciprocated. The dictates of absolute morality are repeatedly shown to be an uncertain guide to conduct in the real world, where the best motives may lead to the worst outcomes. Mme de Clèves's confession destroys her husband, but the tragedy is ultimately attributable to Mme de Chartres, 'a woman of outstanding goodness, virtue and merit', motivated by the apparently laudable desire to find a suitable match for her daughter and to protect her against the pitfalls of love.

Moral absolutes may seem to apply equally to men and women, but the novel recognizes a force in social relations that goes beyond 'virtue' and morality. While there is no danger to Nemours in revealing his desire for Mme de Clèves, for her to show her intimate feelings in the public domain would be to breach a taboo. It is a similar taboo – indicated by the stress on the exceptional nature of what she is doing – that she disregards in her confession to her husband and later, fully accepting the consequences, in her final conversation with Nemours. The penalty in the first instance is the death of her husband, in the second her own. And, while the writer asserts the importance of women in the social and political spheres, at a court where politics is undissociable from love, she does not imply that men and women participate on equal terms. A woman must either preserve the divide between her public face and private thoughts, or perish. In this unequal contest, it is not sincerity, but the balanced separation between public and private beings that helps a woman to achieve the ideal state of *repos*.

A similar precarious balance is reflected in the political sphere, which thus becomes continuous with the private one. Henri II, a monarch faithful in his love for one woman, married to another, addicted to outward show, has contrived to keep peace among the potentially hostile factions at court. Of the minor characters in the novel who represent these factions, only two stand out: the Reine Dauphine (Mary Stuart), a vivid portrait of a young woman who loves teasing and fun; and the Vidame de Chartres, hopelessly enmeshed in his romantic intrigues. Both act as foils for the two central characters, the Dauphine bringing out the youth and vivacity of Mme de Clèves, the Vidame showing Nemours's essentially frivolous attitude to romantic affairs. They are, as it were, respectively what Mme de Clèves and M. de Nemours would be, were they not carried away by their passion for each other.

Yet neither the Reine Dauphine nor the Vidame de Chartres was destined for any happy fate. The novelist's view of happiness is as ambivalent as her view of love. Even the ideal that Mme de Chartres recommends to her daughter, of loving one's husband and being loved by him, appears unattainable, since the outcome of Mme de Clèves's education teaches her that a man's love cannot survive possession. The tranquillity she ultimately achieves is the result of renunciation, and indistinguishable from death. Perhaps the most puzzling aspect of this work is that cold message, expressed in the austere dialect of French classical literature; because *The Princesse de Clèves* is moving precisely by its refusal of excess in the expression of emotion, and attests to the permanence of those feelings that its heroine renounces out of a conviction that they cannot endure.

The more one considers the moral of this book, the less 'moral' it seems. Like affairs of state, which are subject to sudden and disastrous change as the result of a trivial accident such as the death of Henri II, the lives of individuals are tragically determined by fate and by circumstance. Within these constraints, people act, driven by egotism and impulse, rather than by virtue or moral imperatives, and are punished for disregard of social, rather than religious taboos. If Mme de Clèves is heroic, it is not because she is virtuous, but because in the end she chooses the one course that will permit her to preserve her integrity and to remain, relatively, free. She is the heroine of her story, in fact, for no other reason than that she is the central consciousness around which the rest revolve, led by her feelings but not blinded by them. She alone is allowed to share her creator's sense of irony; and while Nemours may laugh at the ridiculous entanglements of his friend the Vidame de Chartres, only she, at a moment of the most intense emotion, seeing her lover, the handsomest of all the handsome men at court and almost irresistible to women, fall on his knees in front of her, could smile at the scene before, a few minutes later, walking triumphantly out of the room.

A Note on the Translation

The Princesse de Clèves was published anonymously by Claude Barbin in 1678 in four volumes. There were several re-editions, some pirated, but the text presents relatively few problems for a work of the period. This translation was made from the edition first published by Garnier-Flammarion in 1966, and I have referred to others, including the one in Éditions de la Pléiade, to which I am indebted for some of the information in the notes.

The first translation of the novel for Penguin Classics was done in 1950 by Nancy Mitford, and she agreed that it should be republished with revisions by Leonard Tancock in 1978. Tancock, in his 'Note on the Revision of This Text', was dismissive of Nancy Mitford's work, saying that she 'made no pretence of strict academic accuracy', and pointing to specific cases of omissions, telescoping, ignorance of seventeenth-century usage, additions, slips, errors and misprints in her translation.

At base, Tancock and Mitford had quite opposite views of their task. For Tancock, the translator's duty is solely towards the work, and 'he' (Tancock's pronoun) has no right to take liberties by paraphrasing, omissions, explanatory additions or changes of order. Mitford, on the other hand, considered that her primary duty was towards the reader: if she felt that one adjective sounded better than Mme de Lafayette's two, she had no scruples about the omission, and she would add a phrase here and there for the sake of clarity. For the reader's convenience, she also divided the book into chapters and, overall, produced a very fluent version with a distinctive tone of voice, which lasted well over the forty years after it first appeared.

For myself, I have no definite opinion in this argument between the letter and the spirit. While I sympathize with Mitford's search for readability and believe that a translator must produce a clear text that is comprehensible to the reader, this obviously does not excuse errors or gratuitous omissions; and I should feel uncomfortable in making any significant adjustments to the text just for the sake of convenience. In this sense, it is Mitford who appears condescending, in her assumption that the reader expects a seventeenth-century novel to be no more demanding than a twentieth-century one. And her translation, while it catches some qualities of the original (lightness of touch, at times a certain archness of tone), does so at a price. She succeeded in producing a version of *The Princesse de Clèves* which an English reader of the twentieth century can enjoy, but which sacrifices something in order to naturalize Mme de Lafayette's book.

This is an entirely new version, which attempts to reconcile fidelity to both the letter and the spirit of Mme de Lafayette's novel. Her language was seventeenth-century French and mine is twentieth-century English: I have tried to suggest that the passage from one to the other is not altogether straight-forward. I hope that I have retained a sense of the novel's distance in language and time, and that the reader will suc-cumb to the enduring appeal of the work, while appreciating at the same time the extent to which it belongs in the par-ticular context of French classical literature.

I have added as few notes as possible. Information on the historical background and personalities has been grouped in the first six notes, where it will be easy to find. I preferred this solution to the alphabetical list of personalities attached, in place of end-notes, to the previous Penguin translation.

The Princesse de Cléves

BOOK ONE

———◆———

At no time in France were splendour and refinement so brilliantly displayed as in the last years of the reign of Henri II.[1] The monarch was courteous, handsome and fervent in love: though his passion for Diane de Poitiers, Duchesse de Valentinois,[1] had lasted for above twenty years, it was no less ardent, and the tokens he gave of it were no less exquisite.

Since he excelled at every sort of physical exercise, he made that his main occupation. Every day there was hunting and tennis, dancing, tilting at rings or similar pastimes. The colours and ciphers of Mme de Valentinois were everywhere to be seen, as she was herself, attired in a manner that might have befitted her grand-daughter, Mlle de la Marck, who was then of marriageable age.

Her presence was warranted by that of the Queen. The King's consort was beautiful, though no longer in the first flush of youth. She loved splendour, magnificence and pleasure. The King had married her when still Duc d'Orléans and younger brother of the Dauphin who died at Tournon — a crown prince whose birth and noble qualities had marked him as worthy to succeed his father, King François I.

The Queen's ambitious temperament made her delight to rule. She seemed easily to endure the King's attachment to the Duchesse de Valentinois and gave no sign of jealousy; but it was hard to fathom her true feelings, since she was most proficient at disguising them and policy required her to support the proximity of the duchess, if she was to enjoy that of the King. He delighted in the conversation of women, even those with whom he was not in love: every day, he visited the

Queen at the hour when she received and when all that was most handsome and most elegant, of either sex, would not fail to attend.

Never has any court possessed so many lovely women and admirably handsome men: it seemed as though Nature had delighted in endowing the greatest of the nobility with her finest gifts. Mme Elisabeth de France,[2] later Queen of Spain, had started to exhibit astounding wit and the incomparable beauty that was to prove so fatal to her. Mary Stuart,[2] Queen of Scotland, who had just married the Dauphin and was called the Reine Dauphine, was perfection, both in mind and in body. She had been educated at the French court, and entirely adopted its manners; and she had such an innate natural disposition for the finest things that, despite her extreme youth, she enjoyed and appreciated them better than anyone. The Queen, her mother-in-law, and Madame,[2] the King's sister, also loved poetry, drama and music. The late King François I's liking for poetry and letters still exercised a powerful influence in France; and since the King, his son, delighted in bodily sports, every pleasure was to be found at his court. But it owed its splendour and majesty to the vast number of princes and peers of exceptional quality: those I shall name were, in their different ways, the ornament and wonder of their age.

The King of Navarre[3] enjoyed universal respect for the nobility of his rank and character. He excelled in war; and the Duc de Guise[3] inspired him with such a spirit of rivalry that several times he had been impelled to give up his place among the generals and fight beside Guise as a common soldier, in the most dangerous parts of the field. It is true that the duke had shown proof of such astounding valour and gained such triumphs that there can have been none among the foremost officers who did not wish to rival him. His valour was complemented by every other quality: he had a great depth of understanding, a noble and elevated soul, and equal ability both in war and in the affairs of state. His brother, the Cardinal de Lorraine,[3] had been born with immoderate ambition, a lively mind and wonderful eloquence.

He had acquired a depth of learning that he employed to enhance his prestige by defending the Catholic faith, which was at that time starting to come under attack. His other brother, the Chevalier de Guise,[3] later known as the Grand Prieur, was universally loved, comely, witty, adroit and celebrated throughout Europe for his valour. The Prince de Condé[3] had a small and ill-favoured body, but within it a mighty and proud soul, and a wit that endeared him to even the most beautiful of women.

The Duc de Nevers,[4] whose life had been made glorious by war and by the offices of state that he had held, though somewhat advanced in age, delighted the court. He had three perfectly well-favoured sons. The second, known as the Prince de Clèves,[4] was worthy of his glorious name: he was brave and generous, and prudent beyond his years. The Vidame de Chartres,[4] heir to that ancient House of Vendôme whose name even the princes of the royal blood have not been ashamed to bear, was equally distinguished in the arts of war and those of peace. A handsome man, he exhibited the most powerful and brilliant qualities: pleasant features, valour, boldness and liberality.

In short, if there was anyone who might be compared to the Duc de Nemours,[4] he alone could bear the comparison. But Nemours was nature's masterpiece: his least striking attribute was to be the most handsome and comely of men. Where he excelled above all others was in his incomparable valour and a distinction of mind, features and manners that belonged only to him. His spirited temperament was equally fascinating to both men and women, he showed extraordinary skill in all that he did and set a fashion of dress that was followed by everyone, but could not be imitated; in brief, his whole being had a presence which ensured that wherever he appeared, all eyes were drawn to him. There was no lady in the court whose pride would not have been flattered, were he to feel some attachment for her; few of those to whom he had become attached could boast that they had resisted him; and there were even several for whom he had shown no tender feelings who had not relented in their passion for him. He had such gentleness and such a gallant nature that he was unable to deny some consideration to those who sought his regard. Consequently he had many mistresses, but it was hard to discern which of them he truly loved. He often visited the Reine Dauphine: her beauty, her sweet nature, her readiness to please and the particular esteem that she manifested towards the duke, often gave reason to think that he even aspired to her favours. Her uncles, the Guise brothers, had risen considerably in rank and estimation by her marriage; they were ambitious, seeking to equal the princes of the blood and to share the power of the Connétable de Montmorency,[5] to whom the King entrusted most of the conduct of affairs. He treated the Duc de Guise and the Maréchal de Saint-André[5] as his favourites, but those whom royal favour or the affairs of state brought close to the King might only remain there by deferring to the Duchesse de Valentinois. Though she was no longer possessed of either youth or beauty, she ruled him with an authority so absolute that she might be said to be mistress at once of his person and of the State.

The King had always loved the Connétable and, as soon as he ascended the throne, recalled him from the exile into which he had been sent by King François I. The court was divided between the Guise brothers and the Connétable, who had the support of the royal princes. Each faction continually sought to win over the Duchesse de Valentinois. The Duc de Guise's brother, the Duc d'Aumale, had married one of her daughters and the Connétable had ambitions to conclude a similar match. He was not satisfied with having married his eldest son to Diane, daughter of the King and of a Piedmontese lady (who entered a convent immediately after the birth). There had been many obstacles to this match, because of the promises young Montmorency had made to Mlle de Piennes, one of the Queen's ladies-in-waiting; and, though the King had shown extraordinary patience and goodwill in surmounting them, the Connétable did not feel secure unless he had the support of the Duchesse de Valentinois and had

estranged her from the Guises, whose eminence was starting
to give the duchess cause for anxiety. She had delayed the
Dauphin's marriage with the Queen of Scots for as long as
she could: she found it equally hard to endure the young
Queen's beauty, her wit and intelligence, and the advancement
the marriage had conferred on Mary's uncles, the Guise
brothers. She particularly disliked the Cardinal de Lorraine:
he had spoken to her with sarcasm, even with contempt. She
could see that he was attaching himself to the Queen, with
the result that the Connétable found her disposed to take his
side and ally herself to him by a marriage between Mlle de la
Marck, her grand-daughter, and his younger son, M. d'Anville (who subsequently succeeded him in the office of Connétable, under Charles IX). As far as the Connétable could see,
there were no objections on d'Anville's part to the match,
such as he had encountered with Montmorency. But, though
the reason was unknown to him, the difficulties were no less
great. M. d'Anville was hopelessly in love with the Dauphine
and, slight though his hopes must be from this attachment,
he could not be resolved to enter into a commitment that
would divide his attentions.

The Maréchal de Saint-André was the only member of the
court who belonged to no faction. He was among the favourites of the King, who was attracted solely by his personal
qualities: he had been loved by the King before his accession
and, after that, made Maréchal de France at an age when
much lesser honours are seldom bestowed. The royal favour
elevated him to a position that he maintained through his
own merits and his personal charm, the superb refinement of
his table and his furnishings, and the greatest liberality ever
seen in a private individual. The King's generosity supplied
this expenditure: he was generous to a fault with those whom
he loved and, though he did not possess every great quality,
he had many, above all a love and understanding of war.
Consequently, he had many successes and, if we exclude the
Battle of Saint-Quentin, his reign had been a succession
of victories.[6] He had personally won the Battle of Renti,

Piedmont had been conquered, the English had been driven from France and the Emperor Charles V had seen the collapse of his fortunes before the city of Metz, which he had fruitlessly besieged with all the forces of the Empire and of Spain. Nonetheless, as the mishap at Saint-Quentin had diminished our hopes of conquest and as, since that time, fortune had seemed to favour the two Kings equally, they found themselves imperceptibly drawn towards peace.

The dowager Duchesse de Lorraine had started to propose it at the time of the Dauphin's marriage, since when there had been constant secret negotiations. Finally, Cercamp, in the Artois region, was chosen for the meeting-place. The Cardinal de Lorraine, the Connétable de Montmorency and the Maréchal de Saint-André represented the King; the Duc d'Albe and the Prince d'Orange, Philip II; and the Duc and Duchesse de Lorraine acted as intermediaries. The main clauses concerned the marriage of Elisabeth de France to Don Carlos, Infante of Spain, and that of Madame, the King's sister, with the Duc de Savoie.

However, the King remained at the frontier, where he received news of the death of Mary, Queen of England. He dispatched the Comte de Randan to Elizabeth, to congratulate her on her accession, and he was joyfully received. Elizabeth's right to the succession was questionable, so it was beneficial to her to have it acknowledged by the King. The count found her well-informed about the politics of the French court and the merits of its courtiers; but, most of all, he found her so full of the reputation of the Duc de Nemours, she spoke to him so often about this nobleman and with such zeal that, on his return, when he came to give a report of his journey to the King, he told him that there was nothing to which Nemours might not aspire in respect of the English Queen, and that he had no doubt she might be prepared to marry him. The King spoke to Nemours that same evening, asking Randan to give an account of all his conversations with Elizabeth and advising Nemours to try for this great fortune. At first, the duke thought that the King could not be in earnest, but observing the contrary:

'At least, sire,' he said, 'if I am to undertake such an uncertain enterprise on the advice and in the service of Your Majesty, I beg him to keep it secret until success has justified it in public opinion, and not to let me be seen as vain enough to imagine that a Queen who has never seen me, should wish to marry me for love.'

The King promised to speak to no one except the Connétable, actually considering that secrecy was vital to the success of the plan. M. de Randan advised M. de Nemours to go to England on the pretext of mere travel, but the duke could not make up his mind to it. Instead, he sent his favourite, Lignerolles, a capable young man, to determine the Queen's feelings and attempt to begin the courtship. While awaiting the outcome of this mission, he went to see the Duc de Savoie, who was then in Brussels with the Spanish King. The death of Queen Mary had brought considerable obstacles to peace. The assembly dissolved at the end of November and the King returned to Paris.

There then appeared at court a beauty who attracted every eye; and it must be supposed that she exhibited true perfection, since she inspired awe in a place where people were so much accustomed to the sight of beauty. One of the greatest heiresses in France, she was from the same house as the Vidame de Chartres. Her father had died young, leaving her in the care of his wife, Mme de Chartres, a woman of outstanding goodness, virtue and merit. After she lost her husband, it was many years before she returned to court. During this time, she devoted herself to the upbringing of her daughter, concerned with the cultivation of her mind and her appearance, while taking care also to make her virtuous and worthy of love. Most mothers believe that, to protect young people, it is enough to refrain from speaking about matters of the heart in front of them. Mme de Chartres held the opposite view. She often described love to her daughter, showing her all its attractions, the more easily to persuade her of its dangers; she told her of men's lack of sincerity, their deceit and their unfaithfulness; and of the domestic misfortunes occasioned by liaisons. And she showed her, on the other hand, how much tranquillity attached to the life of a respectable woman, and how much brilliance and grandeur might accrue to one who already possessed both beauty and birth, by the addition of virtue; but she also showed her how difficult it was to preserve that virtue, other than through extreme self-discipline and scrupulous dedication to that which, alone, can make for the happiness of a woman: namely, to love her husband and to be loved by him.

This heiress was at that time one of the most eligible women in France and, although very young, had received many proposals of marriage. Mme de Chartres, who was exceptionally proud, considered almost nothing worthy of her daughter and, now that she was in her sixteenth year, wished to bring her to court. When she arrived, the Vidame went before her: he was surprised by the great beauty of Mlle de Chartres, and had good reason to be so. The whiteness of her complexion and her blonde hair gave her an unparalleled radiance; all her features were regular and both her face and her figure full of grace and charm.

The day after her arrival, she went to match some precious stones at the house of an Italian who dealt in such things for everybody. This man had arrived from Florence with the Queen and become so rich from his dealings that his house seemed rather that of a nobleman than a merchant. While she was there, the Prince de Clèves came in. He was so astonished by her beauty that he could not hide his surprise, nor could Mlle de Chartres prevent herself from blushing when she saw the effect she was having upon him. However, she rapidly recovered, betraying no greater interest in the prince than good manners would require towards a man of his evident rank. M. de Clèves looked at her in admiration, unable to imagine who this lovely person could be that he did not know. From her deportment and from those who attended her, he realized that she must be someone of the highest rank. She was so young that he supposed her to be an unmarried woman, but since he could see no mother with her, and the Italian (who was also unacquainted with her) called her 'madame', he did not know what to think and continued to stare at her with amazement. He observed that his look was embarrassing her (which is not usually the case with young people, always delighted to see the impression made by their beauty); he even felt that he must be the cause of her impatience to be gone and she did, indeed, leave in quite a short time. M. de Clèves consoled himself for losing her from sight with the expectation that he could learn who she was, but he was very surprised to discover that nobody could enlighten him. He remained so moved by her beauty and the modest demeanour that he had observed in her, that one might also say he conceived an extraordinary passion and regard for her from that very moment. The same evening, he went to call on Madame, the King's sister.

This princess was most highly thought of, thanks to her influence over her brother, the King. This was so great that the King, when the peace treaty was being signed, agreed to return Piedmont so that she could marry the Duc de Savoie. Although she had wished all her life to get married, she only wanted to marry a sovereign: this was the reason that she turned down the King of Navarre when he was still Duc de Vendôme, and had always wished for M. de Savoie. She had a predilection for him since seeing him in Nice at the meeting between King François I and Pope Paul III. Possessing wit and a discerning taste for beautiful things, she attracted all that was finest to her house. At certain times the whole court was there.

M. de Clèves arrived as usual, but so full of the wit and beauty of Mlle de Chartres that he could not speak of anything else. He recounted the afternoon's events to the company and did not tire of praising this young lady that he had seen, even though he did not know who she was. Madame replied that there was no one corresponding to his description and that, had there been, everyone would have recognized her. Mme de Dampierre, her lady-in-waiting and the friend of Mme de Chartres, hearing this conversation, went up to the princess and whispered that the person M. de Clèves had seen was undoubtedly Mlle de Chartres. Madame turned to him and said that, if he wished to return there the following day, she would introduce him to this young woman who had made such an impression on him. And so it was: Mlle de Chartres appeared the next day and was received by the two Queens with every mark of condescension, and by everyone with such admiration that wherever she went, she heard only praise. She accepted it with such noble modesty that it seemed either that she did not hear those compliments or, at least, that she was unaffected by them. She then went to visit Madame, the King's sister who, after praising her beauty, told her of the effect she had produced on M. de Clèves. A moment later, the prince himself came in:

'Come,' Madame told him, 'and judge whether I have kept my word and whether, by here showing you Mlle de Chartres, I am not bringing before you that beauty whom you sought. You may thank me, at least, for having told her of the admiration she has already inspired in you.'

M. de Clèves was overjoyed to see that the same lady whom he had found so prepossessing was of a rank commensurate with her beauty. He went up to her and begged her to remember that he had been the first to admire her and, even before knowing her, had had towards her all the feelings of respect and esteem that she deserved.

He left Madame's together with his friend the Chevalier de Guise. At first, they were unrestrained in their praise of Mlle de Chartres. At length, each felt that he was praising her excessively, so they ceased to say what they thought of her; but they felt obliged to speak of her during the following days whenever they met. For a long time this new beauty was the subject of every conversation. The Queen was most complimentary about her and considerate towards her. The Reine Dauphine made a favourite of her and asked Mme de Chartres to bring her often to visit. The King's daughters sent for her to join in all their entertainments. In short, she was loved and admired by the whole court, except Mme de

Valentinois. Not that the latter was jealous of her beauty, knowing from long experience that she had nothing to fear as far as the King was concerned; but she deeply hated the Vidame de Chartres, whom she had hoped to attach to her own family by the marriage of one of his daughters, and who had instead joined the Queen's faction; so she could not look with favour on someone who bore his name and to whom he demonstrated so great an attachment.

The Prince de Clèves fell passionately in love with Mlle de Chartres and passionately desired to marry her, but he was afraid that Mme de Chartres's pride might be offended were she to give her daughter to a man who was not the eldest son of his house. Yet this house was so eminent, and the Comte d'Eu, the eldest son, had just married a lady so close to the royal family that the prince's misgivings were attributable rather to the diffidence of love than to any rational cause. He had many rivals, of whom the Chevalier de Guise seemed the most to be feared, because of his birth, his personal qualities and the rank that royal favour bestowed on his family. He had fallen in love with Mlle de Chartres at first sight, and was aware of M. de Clèves's feelings, just as M. de Clèves was aware of the Chevalier's. Though they were friends, this aspiring to the same hand had put a barrier between them, so that they could not discuss their feelings, and their friendship had cooled without either having the strength to explain himself to the other. M. de Clèves's fortune, in being the first to see Mlle de Chartres, appeared a good omen which he thought might give him some advantage over his rivals. But he anticipated strong opposition from his father, the Duc de Nevers. The latter was closely associated with the Vidame's enemy, the Duchesse de Valentinois, and this was reason enough for the Duc de Nevers to refuse his consent to a match between his son and the Vidame's niece.

Mme de Chartres, who had been so careful to educate her daughter, continued to show the same concern for her virtue in a place where it was so much needed, being full of so many dangerous examples. Ambition and gallantry were the heart

and soul of the court, preoccupying men and women equally.
There were so many different factions and parties, and the
women played so great a role in them, that love was always
allied to politics and politics to love. No one was untroubled
or unmoved: each considered how to advance, to flatter, to
serve or to harm; boredom and idleness were unknown, since
everyone was engaged in intrigue or the pursuit of pleasure.
The ladies opted for the Queen, the Reine Dauphine, the
Queen of Navarre,[7] Madame, the King's sister, or the Duchesse de Valentinois: these partialities were decided by personal
preference, convention or temperament. Those who had
reached a certain age and professed stricter morals, belonged
to the Queen's party, while the younger women, in search of
frivolity and love, paid court to the Reine Dauphine. The
Queen of Navarre also had her favourites; she was young
and could sway her husband, who gained much influence
through his support for the Connétable. Madame, the King's
sister, was still beautiful and attracted several ladies to her
side. And the Duchesse de Valentinois could have any that she
deigned to notice; but few women appealed to her and, apart
from one or two who enjoyed her friendship and trust, and
whose temperament was compatible with her own, she would
only receive ladies on those days when she felt inclined to
hold court in the same style as the Queen.

All these different factions competed jealously, and the
ladies who belonged to them also rivalled one another in the
contest for favours or for lovers. Considerations of status
and rank were often confused with these others which, less
important though they might be, were no less keenly felt.
There was thus a sort of ordered turbulence at court which
made it delightful, but very dangerous for a young person.
Mme de Chartres was aware of the danger and considered
nothing except how she might protect her daughter against it.
She implored her, not as a mother but as a friend, to confide
every amorous remark that might be addressed to her, and
promised to guide her conduct in situations which are often
embarrassing to the young.

The Chevalier de Guise made so little attempt to disguise
his feelings and intentions regarding Mlle de Chartres that
they were known to everybody. However, he could himself
see only the obstacles to what he desired, knowing very well
that his was not a match that would meet with the approval
of Mme de Chartres, because he lacked the wealth to sustain
his rank; and he knew also that his brothers would not approve of him marrying, because of the lowering in status that
the marriage of younger brothers commonly inflicts on great
families.[8] The Cardinal de Lorraine soon confirmed that he
was not mistaken, condemning his open partiality for Mlle de
Chartres with extraordinary vehemence, though without telling him the true reason for his disapproval: the cardinal
secretly hated the Vidame, though it was only later that this
became public. He would have consented to any match for
his brother rather than one with the Vidame's family, and he
declared the strength of his opposition so openly that Mme
de Chartres was greatly offended, and at pains to demonstrate
that the cardinal had nothing to fear, since she was not
considering such a match. The Vidame adopted the same
stance and was still more offended by that of the cardinal
than was Mme de Chartres, being more aware of its cause.

The Prince de Clèves had not given any less public signs of
his feelings than the Chevalier de Guise. The Duc de Nevers
was pained to learn of his attachment, but thought that if he
were to talk to his son, this would suffice to alter his mind; so
he was very surprised at finding him firmly set on marriage
with Mlle de Chartres. He rebuked him for it, lost his temper
and made so little attempt to disguise his fury that the matter
was soon discussed at court and even reached Mme de
Chartres. She had never doubted that M. de Nevers would
consider marriage with her daughter as advantageous to his
son. She was amazed that both the Clèves family and the
Guises should fear an alliance with her, instead of welcoming
it. The resulting vexation made her seek a match that would
place her daughter above those who considered themselves
placed above her. After weighing all possibilities, she fixed on

the son of the Duc de Montpensier. He was of marriageable age, and the highest in rank at court. Since Mme de Chartres was an intelligent woman, helped by the Vidame who was much in favour, and since her daughter was in reality very eligible, she proceeded with such skill and success that M. de Montpensier appeared to desire the match and it seemed there could be no obstacle to it.

The Vidame, who knew of M. d'Anville's attachment to the Reine Dauphine, decided that he must use her influence with d'Anville to enlist his services on Mlle de Chartres's behalf, with the King and with his close friend, the Prince de Montpensier. He mentioned this to the Reine Dauphine and found her delighted to participate in an affair involving the advancement of someone towards whom she was very well-disposed. She said as much to the Vidame and assured him that, though she knew that her support would displease her uncle, the Cardinal de Lorraine, she would happily overlook this, since she had reason to complain of the cardinal, who daily sided with the Queen against her own interests.

Those of a romantic disposition are always pleased at finding any excuse to speak with their lovers. As soon as the Vidame had left the Reine Dauphine, she called Chastelart,[9] M. d'Anville's favourite (and so acquainted with his passion for her), and told him to give d'Anville the message that he should be at the Queen's that evening. Chastelart was delighted and flattered to accept this commission: he was a gentleman from a good family in Dauphiné whose qualities and intelligence were superior to his birth, allowing him to be received and well treated by all the great noblemen at court: the patronage of the Montmorencys had particularly recommended him to M. d'Anville. He was handsome and athletic, had a pleasant singing voice, wrote verse and possessed a refined and passionate nature which appealed so much to d'Anville that he confided to him his love for the Reine Dauphine. This confidence brought Chastelart close to the princess and, seeing her often, he began to feel the unfortunate passion that was to deprive him of reason, and eventually of life itself.

That evening d'Anville made sure to attend the Queen's, happy that the Reine Dauphine should have chosen him to undertake a mission on her behalf and promising to obey her orders to the letter. But Mme de Valentinois, forewarned about this proposed marriage, had done her best to prevent it, turning the King's mind so firmly against the idea that, when M. d'Anville spoke to him on the matter, he indicated his opposition and even ordered him to inform the Prince de Montpensier of this. One can imagine Mme de Chartres's feelings at the collapse of a plan she ardently desired to succeed, since its failure was so advantageous to her enemies and so detrimental to her daughter.

The Reine Dauphine showed great consideration towards Mlle de Chartres, expressing her regret at having been unable to help:

'As you see,' she told her, 'my power is limited. The Queen and the Duchesse de Valentinois hate me so much that it is difficult to prevent them thwarting me at every turn, either themselves or through those who serve them. Despite which,' she added, 'I have never sought anything except to please them, and they hate me solely on account of the Queen, my mother, who used at one time to give them cause for disquiet and jealousy. The King loved her before Mme de Valentinois, and in the early years of his marriage, when he was still childless, seemed almost prepared to divorce and marry my mother, despite the love he already felt for Mme de Valentinois. She feared a woman whom he had previously loved, whose beauty and wit might outshine her, and so joined forces with the Connétable who was equally opposed to the King marrying a sister of the Guise brothers. They won over the late King despite his bitter hatred of Mme de Valentinois, and, since he loved the Queen, he supported them in preventing the King's divorce. But, to remove any thought he might have of marrying my mother, they arranged for her to be married to the King of Scotland, widower of the King's sister, Mme Magdeleine: they did this because the Scottish King was closer to concluding the match, and so broke their undertakings to the King of England who ardently desired her. This breach of their undertaking almost led to a breach in relations between the two monarchs. Henry VIII was unable to resign himself to not having married my mother and, whatever other French princess was offered him, always said that she could never replace the one that had been snatched away. My mother was indeed a perfect beauty; and it is a remarkable fact that three Kings should have wished to wed her, the widow of a Duc de Longueville. It was her misfortune to have ended with the least among them, in a kingdom where she was only to find unhappiness. It is said that I am like her. I am afraid that I may also resemble her in misfortune, and whatever happiness fate may seem to be preparing for me, I cannot believe that I shall enjoy it.' Mlle de Chartres told the Queen that these sad forebodings were so ill-founded that she would not feel them for long, and that she had no doubt the Queen's good fortune would be as real as it appeared.

From then on, no one dared consider Mlle de Chartres, for fear of displeasing the King or thinking that they might not succeed with somebody who had aspired to marry a prince of the blood. M. de Clèves was restrained by no such considerations. As the death of his father, the Duc de Nevers, occurred around the same time,[10] he was entirely free to follow his heart and, as soon as the proper period of mourning had passed, thought of nothing except how he might marry Mlle de Chartres. He was happy to be able to propose the match now that circumstances had removed the other pretenders to her hand, virtually ensuring that he would not be refused. The only flaw in his happiness was the fear that she might not find him to her liking, and he would have preferred the good fortune of being loved by her to the certainty of marriage without it.

The Chevalier de Guise had caused him some jealousy, but it was inspired more by Guise's qualities than any act on the part of Mlle de Chartres, so he was concerned only to discover whether he was fortunate enough to enjoy her approval of his proposal. He only saw her at the Queens' houses or in public assemblies, where it was difficult to engage her in private conversation. Yet he found the means to do so and, with the greatest possible respect, declared his intentions and his passion. He begged her to tell him her feelings towards him and said that his own were of such a kind that he would be eternally miserable were she to submit to her mother's wishes from duty alone.

Since Mlle de Chartres had the finest and noblest of hearts, she was touched with genuine gratitude at the prince's manner of proceeding. This gratitude imparted a certain tenderness of tone to the words of her reply that was enough to raise the hopes of a man so utterly in love as M. de Clèves, and he was led to believe he had obtained part of what he desired.

She recounted this conversation to her mother. Mme de Chartres told her that there were such fine and good qualities in M. de Clèves and that he gave evidence of such good sense for his age that if her daughter's feelings inclined her to marry him, she would happily consent. Mlle de Chartres replied that she, too, had observed the same qualities in him, and even felt less disinclination to marry him than any other man, but that she was not particularly attracted to him.

The next day, his proposal was communicated to Mme de Chartres and she accepted it, not fearing that, in giving her daughter to the Prince de Clèves, she was giving her to a man whom she could not love. The contract was drawn up, the King informed and the engagement publicly made known.

M. de Clèves was happy, though not fully satisfied. He was much distressed to see that Mlle de Chartres's feelings did not go beyond respect and gratitude: he could not delude himself that she was hiding any that were more tender, since their situation was now of a kind that would have allowed her to reveal them without offending her extreme modesty. Hardly a day passed when he did not reproach her with this.

'Is it possible,' he inquired, 'that I can be anything but happy in our engagement? Yet the truth is that I am not. You show me only a kind of courtesy, and I cannot be contented with that. You betray none of the impatience, anxiety or turmoil of love and are no more moved by my passion than you would be by an attachment founded, not on the allurements of your person, but merely on those of your wealth.'

'It is unjust in you to complain,' she replied. 'I do not know what more you could wish of me and I think propriety does not permit me to go any further than I do.'

'It is true,' he agreed, 'that you accord me certain outward signs, and I should be happy with these if there were anything beneath. But it is not that convention restrains you: it alone dictates your behaviour. I have no effect on your inclinations or your heart, and you experience neither pleasure nor agitation when I am near you.'

'You can surely not doubt,' she returned, 'that I feel joy when I see you; and I blush so often when I do so, that you cannot doubt, either, that the sight of you disturbs me.'

'I am not deceived by your blushes,' he said. 'They derive from feelings of modesty, not from those of the heart, and afford me no greater satisfaction than they ought.'

Mlle de Chartres was at a loss to reply, such distinctions being outside her experience. M. de Clèves saw only too well how far she was from feeling the emotions towards him that he wished, and concluded that she actually did not understand them.

The Chevalier de Guise returned from a journey a few days before the wedding. He had seen so many insurmountable obstacles to his hopes of marrying Mlle de Chartres that he could not delude himself into thinking that they would succeed; yet, despite that, he was deeply pained at seeing her become the wife of another. This anguish did not quell his passion and he remained no less in love. Mlle de Chartres had been aware of his feelings for her. On his return, he let her know that she was responsible for the extreme sadness on his face; and so great were his qualities and his charm that it was difficult to make him unhappy without experiencing some pity for him, so she could not avoid feeling it. But this pity did not produce any further emotion in her; she told her mother about the distress that his affection caused her.

Mme de Chartres marvelled at her daughter's frankness and had good reason to do so, for there was never anyone who possessed so much natural candour. But she was equally impressed by the fact that her heart was not moved, all the more so since she saw very well that the Prince de Clèves had not moved it any more than the rest. For this reason, she took great pains to attach her to her intended husband, and to convince her of the obligation she owed to the partiality he had felt even before knowing her and to the passion he had shown, preferring her to every other match, at a time when no one else dared consider her.

The marriage was solemnized, the ceremony taking place at the Louvre; and in the evening, the King and the Queens came to supper with Mme de Chartres, accompanied by the whole court, and were splendidly entertained. The Chevalier de Guise did not dare make himself conspicuous by not attending, but had so little control over his unhappiness that it was plain to see.

M. de Clèves found Mlle de Chartres unchanged in feeling after her change of name. Being her husband gave him greater rights over her, but not a greater place in his wife's heart. Consequently, even as a husband, he did not cease to be a lover, because he had always something to desire beyond the possession of her; and, though she was entirely correct towards him, he was not entirely satisfied. His violent and uneasy passion for her disturbed his happiness; there was no jealousy to contribute to his anxiety: never has a husband been further from feeling it or a wife from giving him cause. Even so, she was exposed to the society of the court and daily visited the Queens and Madame. All the gallant young men saw her at home or at the house of the Duc de Nevers, her brother-in-law, which was open to everybody. But her manner inspired such respect and was so far from encouraging any advances that the Maréchal de Saint-André, though bold and a protégé of the King, who was moved by her beauty, did not dare show his feelings except by being properly considerate towards her. Several others were in the same case, and Mme de Chartres behaved with such scrupulous regard for every propriety that this, together with her daughter's prudent good sense, made the latter seem unattainable.

The Duchesse de Lorraine was actively arranging peace and also the marriage of her son, the duke. He was betrothed to the King's second daughter, Mme Claude de France, and the wedding was to take place in February.

Meanwhile, the Duc de Nemours had remained in Brussels, his whole time and attention taken up with his plans for England. He constantly received or sent couriers there, his hopes rose daily, and finally Lignerolles informed him that he should go to conclude in person what had started so favourably. He welcomed this news with all the delight of an ambitious young man who sees himself raised to a throne by his mere reputation. His mind had gradually become accustomed to his enormous good fortune and, where he had at first refused to admit it, as something beyond reach, he now expunged the difficulties from his imagination and saw no further obstacle in his path.

He sent post-haste to Paris to order the preparation of a magnificent retinue, so that he might arrive in England with a show appropriate to the great enterprise that brought him there, and hurried back to the court in person to attend the marriage of the Duc de Lorraine.

He arrived the day before the betrothal ceremony and, the same evening, went to inform the King of the state of his affairs, and to learn his commands and advice on what remained to be done. He then went to visit the Queens. Mme de Clèves was not there, so she did not see him or even know of his arrival. But she had heard everyone speak of him as the most handsome and charming nobleman at court: the Dauphine, in particular, had depicted him in such a way and spoken of him so often as to make her curious, even impatient to see him.

She spent the whole day of the betrothal at home preparing herself for the evening's ball and court feast at the Louvre. On her arrival, her beauty and costume were much admired. The ball opened and, while she was dancing with M. de Guise, there was some commotion near the door of the room, as when people make way for someone to enter. Mme de Clèves stopped dancing and, while she was looking around for her next partner, the King called to her to take the person who had just come in. She turned and saw a man whom she thought from the first could only be M. de Nemours, climbing over some seats to get to the dance floor. He was so handsome that it was hard not to be impressed by the first sight of him, especially on that evening, when the care he had taken with his dress added to the natural brilliance of his appearance. But it would have been hard too, to see Mme de Clèves for the first time without being taken aback by her beauty.

M. de Nemours was so captivated by it that, when he was close to her and she was curtsying to him, he could not refrain from exhibiting his admiration. When they started to dance, a murmur of approval rose from the company. The King and the Queens remembered that the pair had never previously met and found it curious to see them dancing, even though they were strangers. When they had finished, they called them over without giving them the opportunity to speak to anyone, and asked if each of them did not want to know who the other was, and whether they had guessed.

'For my part, madame,' said M. de Nemours, 'I have no doubt; but since Mme de Clèves has less cause to guess my name than I to recognize her, I would beg Your Majesty to be kind enough to inform her of it.'

'I think,' said Mme la Dauphine, 'that she knows it as well as you know hers.'

'I assure you, madame,' Mme de Clèves replied, with a slightly embarrassed air, 'that I am not so good as you imagine at divination.'

'You have guessed perfectly well,' the Dauphine retorted, 'and it is even somewhat flattering for M. de Nemours, this refusal to admit that you know him without ever having seen him.'

The Queen interrupted so that the ball could proceed and M. de Nemours danced with the Dauphine. She was a perfect beauty, and had seemed such in M. de Nemours's eyes before he left for Flanders, but throughout that evening he could admire only Mme de Clèves.

The Chevalier de Guise, who still worshipped her, was at her feet, and what had happened gave him acute pain. He considered it an omen that fate destined M. de Nemours to fall in love with Mme de Clèves and, whether he did indeed see some evidence of feeling on her face or whether jealousy showed him more than the truth, he thought that she had been disturbed by the sight of the prince and could not restrain himself from telling her that M. de Nemours was fortunate to have first made her acquaintance in circumstances that were somehow unusual and romantic.

Mme de Clèves returned home, her mind so full of what had happened at the ball that, though it was very late, she went into her mother's room to tell her about it; and she praised M. de Nemours with a particular tone that gave Mme de Chartres the same idea that had occurred to the Chevalier de Guise.

The wedding ceremony took place the next day. Mme de Clèves saw the Duc de Nemours there, with such a charming expression and bearing that she was still more amazed at him.

In the days that followed, she saw him at the Dauphine's, playing tennis with the King and tilting at rings, and she heard him speak. But wherever she saw him, he was so superior to everyone else and so much the focus of every conversation, both because of his manner and his wit, that he rapidly made a profound impression on her.

It is also true that, since M. de Nemours felt a powerful attraction to her which gave him that sweet and lively demeanour that derives from the first impulse to please, he was even more attractive than usual; so that, meeting often and seeing in each other what was most delightful at court, it was inevitable that each should find the other infinitely appealing.

The Duchesse de Valentinois took part in every entertainment and the King showed her the same merry and affectionate attention as in the first days of his passion. Mme de Clèves, who was at a time of life when one refuses to believe a woman can inspire love after the age of twenty-five, was astonished by the King's attachment to the duchess, a grandmother whose grand-daughter had just been married. She often mentioned it to Mme de Chartres:

'Is it possible,' she asked, 'that the King has been in love with her for so long? How can he have formed an attachment with a woman who was much older than himself, who had been his father's mistress and who, so I am told, still has several lovers apart from him?'

'It is true,' her mother answered, 'that the King's passion was not inspired, and did not endure, either because of Mme de Valentinois's merits or because of her fidelity, and it is this that makes it inexcusable. For if that woman had had youth and beauty as well as birth, if she had been virtuous enough to love no one else, if she had loved the King with scrupulous fidelity, and if she had loved him for himself, without consideration of rank or fortune, using her power solely for ends that are worthy or pleasing to the King, one must admit that it would have been hard to begrudge him praise for his great attachment to her. Were I not afraid,' Mme de Chartres went on, 'that you would say of me what everybody says about women of my age, namely that they like to recount stories about their younger days, I should tell you how the King first fell in love with the duchess, and many things to do with the court of the late King which have in fact a considerable bearing on what still happens today.'

'Far from accusing you of telling old stories,' Mme de Clèves replied, 'I might complain that you have not told me the current gossip or informed me of the various interests and liaisons in the court. I am so completely ignorant of them that until a few days ago I imagined M. le Connétable to be on good terms with the Queen.'

'There you were quite mistaken,' said Mme de Chartres. 'The Queen hates the Connétable and if she were ever to acquire any power, he would become only too well aware of that fact. She knows he has often said to the King that, among all his children, only his bastards resembled him.'

'I should never have suspected her hatred for him,' Mme de Clèves interjected, 'seeing how careful the Queen was to write to the Connétable during his imprisonment and the pleasure she expressed on his return, as well as the way that she always addresses him as "*mon compère*" in the same terms as the King does.'

'If you judge by appearances in this place,' said Mme de Chartres, 'you will often be deceived, because what appears to be the case hardly ever is.

'But, to return to Mme de Valentinois: you know that her name is Diane de Poitiers. Her family is very distinguished, deriving from the former dukes of Aquitaine; one of her ancestors was the illegitimate daughter of Louis XI; and, in short, there is only blue blood in her veins. Her father, Saint-Vallier, was implicated in the affair of the Connétable de Bourbon, about which you have heard. He was condemned to be beheaded and led to the scaffold. His daughter, who was extremely beautiful and had already found favour with the late King, succeeded in obtaining her father's life (though I do not know by what means).[11] He was pardoned at a moment when he expected nothing but the axe, but had been so overcome by terror that he collapsed, and a few days later he died. His daughter appeared in court as the King's mistress. His journey to Italy and imprisonment interrupted their affair. When he returned from Spain and Mme la Régente went to meet him at Bayonne, she took all her ladies, including Mlle de Pisseleu, later Duchesse d'Étampes, with whom the King fell in love. She was inferior to Mme de Valentinois in birth, intelligence and beauty: her only advantage was her extreme youth. It has often been said that she was born on the day that Diane de Poitiers was married, but this rumour was inspired by envy, not by the truth, because I am much mistaken if the Duchesse de Valentinois did not marry M. de Brézé, the Grand Sénéchal de Normandie at about the same time as the King fell in love with Mme d'Étampes. There has never been greater antagonism than existed between these two women. The Duchesse de Valentinois could not forgive Mme d'Étampes for having deprived her of the title of King's mistress, and Mme d'Étampes felt violent jealousy towards Mme de Valentinois because the King maintained a relationship with her. He was scrupulously faithful to his mistresses. One always had the title and the honours, but the ladies who were known as belonging to the "little set" took turns with him. He was greatly distressed by the loss of his son, the Dauphin, who died at Tournon and was thought to have been poisoned. He never felt the same affection or fondness for his second son, the present King, not considering him sufficiently bold or vivacious. He complained about it one day to Mme de Valentinois and she told him that she would persuade the prince to fall in love with her, to make him livelier and better company. As you know, she succeeded, and their love has endured for twenty years unaltered by time or other obstacles.

'At first, the late King disapproved, either because he was still enough in love with Mme de Valentinois himself to feel jealous or because he was influenced by the Duchesse d'Étampes, who was in despair at the prospect of the Dauphin forming an alliance with her enemy. Whatever the reason, he certainly viewed this affair with anger and displeasure, and showed it daily. But his son was intimidated neither by his hostility nor by his anger, and nothing could force him to relinquish the attachment or to disguise what he felt: the King had to resign himself to it. Yet this opposition to his wishes estranged him still further from the Dauphin and attached him more strongly to his third son, the Duc d'Orléans, who was a fiery youth, handsome in face and figure, energetic and ambitious, needing restraint, but one who would have made a very great ruler, if age had matured him.

'The Dauphin enjoyed precedence as the elder, and the
Duc d'Orléans enjoying the King's favour meant that there
was a kind of competition between them that amounted to
hostility. This rivalry began when they were children and
never diminished. When the Emperor came to France, he
gave undisguised preference to the Duc d'Orléans over the
Dauphin, and the latter felt this so acutely that when the
Emperor was at Chantilly, he wanted the Connétable to arrest
him without waiting for the King's command. The Connétable refused and the King subsequently criticized him for not
complying with his son's wishes; this had much to do with
the Connétable's dismissal from the court.

'The estrangement between the two brothers gave the Duchesse d'Etampes the idea of gaining the Duc d'Orléans's support
with the King against Mme de Valentinois. She succeeded:
though the prince was not in love with her, he took her side
almost as warmly as the Dauphin did that of Mme de Valentinois,
with the result, as you might imagine, that there were two
factions at court; but these intrigues went deeper than a mere
quarrel between two women.

'The Emperor still felt some partiality for the Duc d'Orléans
and several times offered to cede him the Duchy of Milan. In
the subsequent peace proposals, he offered the prospect that
he might give him the seventeen provinces[12] and his daughter's hand. The Dauphin was opposed both to peace and to
this marriage. He used the Connétable, whom he had always
liked, to convince the King that it was important not to give
his successor a brother as powerful as the Duc d'Orléans
would be, were he to enjoy both an alliance with the Emperor
and the seventeen provinces. The Connétable was only too
happy to follow the Dauphin's wishes, since they were contrary to those of his declared enemy, Mme d'Étampes, who
ardently desired the advancement of the Duc d'Orléans.

'At this time, the Dauphin was commanding the King's
army in Champagne and had reduced the Emperor's forces
to such an extent that they would have perished entirely, had
not the Duchesse d'Étampes feared that such a marked advan-

tage would lead us to refuse peace and the Duc d'Orléans's alliance with the Emperor: so she secretly warned our enemies to make a surprise attack on Épernay and Château-Thierry which were full of provisions. They did so, and by this means saved their entire army.

'The duchess did not benefit long from the success of her treachery. The Duc d'Orléans died shortly afterwards at Farmoutier, from some kind of infectious disease. He loved one of the most beautiful women in the court, and she returned his love. I shall not name her because she has since lived such an exemplary life and taken such care to conceal her love for the prince that her reputation deserves to be protected. By chance, she learned the news of her husband's death on the same day as that of the Duc d'Orléans, so that she had an excuse to conceal her real sorrow without suffering an agony of self-restraint.

'The King did not long survive his son, dying two years later. He recommended the Dauphin to enlist the services of the Cardinal de Tournon and the Amiral d'Annebauld,[13] saying nothing of the Connétable who, as far as he was concerned, had been banished to Chantilly. But the first thing that his son, the present King, did was to recall him and appoint him to manage the affairs of State.

'Mme d'Étampes was dismissed and subjected to all the mistreatment she could expect from an all-powerful enemy: the Duchesse de Valentinois revenged herself fully on her rival and everyone else who had fallen foul of her. Her empire over the King seemed even more absolute than it had when he was still Dauphin. In the twelve years of his reign, she has been the absolute mistress of everything: she has control of appointments and offices; she has banished the Cardinal de Tournon, the Chancellor Olivier and Villeroy. Those who have tried to warn the King against her have been destroyed in the attempt. The Comte de Taix, the Grand Master of Artillery, did not like her and felt constrained to talk about her flirtations, especially with the Comte de Brissac, which had already aroused the King's jealousy. But she arranged for the Comte de Taix to be disgraced and relieved of his office: the most incredible thing is that she arranged for him to be replaced in it by the Comte de Brissac, who was subsequently appointed Maréchal de France. Yet the King's jealousy increased to the point where he could no longer suffer the Maréchal's presence at court; however, jealousy, which is bitter and violent in all other men, is mild in him and moderated by his extraordinary respect for his mistress, so that he only dared remove his rival on the pretext of making him Governor of Piedmont. The Comte de Brissac spent several years there before returning last winter, alleging that he needed troops and other supplies for the army under his command. It may be that one major reason for this journey was the desire to see Mme de Valentinois again and the fear of being forgotten by her. The King received him very coldly. The Guise brothers, who are not fond of him but dare not show it because of Mme de Valentinois, made use of his declared enemy the Vidame to prevent him obtaining any of the things that he had come to request. It was not difficult to harm his interests: the King hated him and was uneasy at his presence. The result was that he had to return empty-handed from his journey, except that he may have revived feelings in the heart of Mme de Valentinois that time had started to extinguish. There are many others who might give the King cause for jealousy, but either he is unaware of them, or has not dared to complain.

'I am not sure, my child,' Mme de Chartres added, 'whether you think I have told you more than you wanted to know.'

'On the contrary,' Mme de Clèves replied, 'that complaint is the last I am inclined to make, and only the fear of wearying you with my importunities restrains me from enquiring about many other matters that you have still not told me.'

At first, M. de Nemours's passion for Mme de Clèves was so strong that he had no interest, or even memory, of those he had previously loved, though he had continued to correspond with them during his absence. He did not even bother to look for any excuse to break off with them: he had not the patience to listen to their pleas and answer their complaints. His passionate feelings for Mme la Dauphine were unable to compete in his heart against Mme de Clèves. Even his impatience to set off for England began to wane and he did not press forward with such enthusiasm in the arrangements for his departure. Because Mme de Clèves often went there, he often went to the Dauphine's and was not sorry that people should continue to assume what they thought were his feelings for the Queen. Mme de Clèves stood so high in his esteem that he decided not to give her any sign of his love, rather than risk it becoming public. He did not even speak of it to the Vidame de Chartres, who was a close friend from whom he kept no secrets. He was so discreet in his manner and so wary that nobody suspected him of being in love with Mme de Clèves, except the Chevalier de Guise. She would have been at pains to detect it herself, were it not that her own feeling for him made her particularly attentive to his behaviour and this left no room for doubt.

She was less disposed to tell her mother her mind about the prince's feelings than she had been in speaking to her of her other admirers: without exactly deciding to conceal anything, she said nothing. But Mme de Chartres perceived it only too clearly, as well as her daughter's liking for him. This knowledge was very painful to her, since she easily judged how dangerous it was for a young woman to be loved by so attractive a man as M. de Nemours when his feelings were reciprocated. Something that happened a few days later entirely confirmed her suspicion that the attraction was mutual.

The Maréchal de Saint-André, who sought every opportunity to exhibit his affluence, using the excuse that he wished to show off his recently completed house, begged the King to do him the honour of taking supper there with the Queens. The Maréchal was also pleased to let Mme de Clèves admire these visible signs of his extravagance, amounting to prodigality.

A few days before the one chosen for this entertainment,

the Dauphin, whose health was weak, fell ill and was receiving no one. The Queen, his wife, spent the whole day at his side. In the evening, since he was better, he admitted all the nobility who had been waiting in his antechamber. The Reine Dauphine returned home and found Mme de Clèves, with some other ladies who were among her closest friends.

Since it was then quite late and she had not dressed, she did not go to the Queen's. She said that she would not go out and called for her jewels, so that she might choose some for the Maréchal's ball and give some to Mme de Clèves to whom she had promised them. While they were engaged in this, the Prince de Condé arrived: his rank allowed him to enter anywhere. The Reine Dauphine told him that he had doubtless come from the house of her husband, the Dauphin, and asked what was happening there.

'They are arguing with M. de Nemours, madame,' he replied. 'And he is putting his case so warmly that he must believe in it. I think he has some mistress or other who must make him uneasy when she is at the ball, because he insists that it is distressing for a lover to see the object of his love on such occasions.'

'What!' the Dauphine exclaimed. 'Does M. de Nemours not want his mistress to go to the ball? I did think that husbands might not want their wives to go there, but I had never imagined that lovers could share that opinion.'

'In M. de Nemours's view,' the Prince de Condé said, 'balls are the most unbearable things for lovers, whether their feelings are returned or not. He claims that, if they are loved, then they have the annoyance of being less loved for several days. There is no woman who is not too preoccupied with her dress and toilet to think about her lover, it consumes all her thoughts. And this concern is with how she appears to anybody, not only to the person she loves; when she is at a ball, she wants to be liked by everyone who sees her, so that if she is pleased with her appearance, she experiences a pleasure for which she is not mainly indebted to her lover. He also says that, when one is not loved, the pain of seeing one's mistress on such public occasions is even greater: the more she is admired by others, the more one feels the misfortune of not being loved, and constantly fears that her beauty will inspire some more fortunate passion than one's own. In short, he considers no affliction comparable to that of seeing one's mistress at a ball, except knowing that she is there, when one is not there oneself.'

Mme de Clèves pretended not to hear what the Prince de Condé was saying, though she was in fact listening attentively. It was not hard for her to guess her own role in M. de Nemours's argument, particularly what he said about the sorrow of not being at a ball when one's mistress was there, since he was to be absent from that held by the Maréchal de Saint-André, the King sending him to meet the Duc de Ferrare.

The Dauphine laughed with the Prince de Condé and disagreed with M. de Nemours.

'There is only one circumstance, madame,' he said, 'when M. de Nemours would permit his mistress to go to a ball, and that is if he were giving it himself; adding that, last year, when he gave one for Your Majesty, he considered his mistress had done him a favour by attending though she seemed only to follow you: it is always a favour to a lover to participate in a pleasure that he is giving; and it is also a pleasant thing for a lover to be observed as master of a place at which the whole court is present, when she sees him successfully doing the honours.'

'M. de Nemours was right,' the Dauphine said, smiling, 'to approve of his mistress going to the ball. On that occasion there were so many women to whom he had given a claim to the title that, if they had not attended, the place would have been almost deserted.'

As soon as the Prince de Condé started to describe M. de Nemours's opinion on the matter, Mme de Clèves experienced a strong disinclination to go to the Maréchal de Saint-André's ball. She easily persuaded herself that she should not in fact go to the house of a man who was in love with her, and was very pleased to find such a proper excuse for doing something that would be a favour to M. de Nemours. Yet, she took away the ornaments given her by the Dauphine; and in the evening, when showing them to her mother, said that she meant not to use them, since the Maréchal de Saint-André was so open in displaying his attachment to her, she had no doubt he would let it be known that she was associated with the entertainment he was offering the King and, with the excuse of being a good host, pay her attentions that might prove embarrassing.

For a while, Mme de Chartres argued against her daughter, finding her reasons odd. But, seeing that she was determined, she agreed and told her that she must pretend to be ill, so as to have some excuse not to go, since no one would support her in her real reason for not going, and indeed no one should be allowed even to suspect it. Mme de Clèves willingly agreed to spend a few days at home, so as to avoid anywhere where she would not find M. de Nemours, and he left without having the pleasure of knowing that she would not be going to the ball.

He returned the day after the event and discovered that she had not attended; but, since he did not know that anyone had told her of his conversation at the Dauphin's, he had no idea of his good fortune in having been the one to prevent her going.

The following day, while he was at the Queen's and was speaking to the Dauphine, Mme de Chartres and Mme de Clèves arrived and went over to her. Mme de Clèves was somewhat casually turned out, like a person who had been ill, but her face belied her dress.

'You look so lovely,' the Dauphine said, 'that I would never believe you had been unwell. I think that the Prince de Condé, when he told you M. de Nemours's views on dancing, convinced you that it would be a favour to the Maréchal de Saint-André if you were to accept his invitation and it was this that prevented you.'

Mme de Clèves blushed at the fact that the Dauphine,

having so perceptively guessed her reason, had mentioned it in front of M. de Nemours.

And at that very moment, Mme de Chartres realized why her daughter had not wished to attend the ball; so, to prevent M. de Nemours reaching the same conclusion, she interrupted with every appearance of speaking the truth.

'I assure you, madame,' she told the Dauphine, 'that Your Majesty gives my daughter more credit than she deserves. She was truly ill; but, if I had not prevented her, I believe she would certainly have accompanied you and shown herself in public, unwell though she was, in order to enjoy all the wonderful things to be seen at yesterday evening's ball.'

The Dauphine believed Mme de Chartres, and M. de Nemours was very annoyed at finding it plausible, though Mme de Clèves blushed in a way that made him suspect the Dauphine's first explanation was not altogether untrue. At first, Mme de Clèves was cross that M. de Nemours might have had reason to think it was because of him that she had not gone to the Maréchal de Saint-André's; but afterwards, she felt a sort of regret that her mother had entirely dispelled that notion.

Although the gathering at Cercamp had dissolved, peace negotiations still continued and took such a course that, at the end of February, a new meeting was convened, at Cateau-Cambrésis. The same delegates attended, and the resulting absence of the Maréchal de Saint-André removed the rival from whom M. de Nemours had most to fear – as much because of his close scrutiny of all those who approached Mme de Clèves as for any progress that he might make in his own courtship of her.

Mme de Chartres did not want to let her daughter see that she understood her feelings for the prince, for fear that she might suspect the motives behind certain things that her mother wanted to tell her. One day, she started to speak about him, in favourable terms, but insidiously praising his good sense, in being unable to fall in love and treating his relations with women as a pleasure, rather than serious attachments. 'This is not to say,' she added, 'that people have not suspected him of having a great passion for the Dauphine; and I see that he often visits her, so I should advise you, as far as possible, to avoid speaking to him, especially in private, since in view of the Dauphine's condescension towards you, people would think you their go-between, and you know how disagreeable it is to be thought that. If the rumour continues, you might go rather less to the Dauphine's, to avoid becoming involved in such affairs.'

Mme de Clèves had never heard speak of M. de Nemours and the Dauphine. She was surprised at what her mother was saying and thought she could see how mistaken she had been in everything she had imagined about the prince's feelings, so that her face fell. Mme de Chartres noticed this. People were coming in at that moment, and Mme de Clèves went and shut herself in her room.

It is impossible to describe the pain she felt on realizing, as a result of what her mother had just told her, how much the Duc de Nemours meant to her: she had not yet dared admit it to herself. She saw then that the feelings she had for him were those that M. de Clèves had so often required of her, and she felt the full shame of experiencing them for someone other than a husband who deserved them. She felt wounded and confused by the fear that M. de Nemours only wished to use her as an excuse in his affair with the Dauphine, and this idea made her determine to tell Mme de Chartres what she had not yet told her.

The following morning she went to her mother's room to do as she had resolved. But she found Mme de Chartres with a slight temperature and not inclined to conversation. However, the illness seemed so mild that Mme de Clèves did not put off attending the Dauphine's after dinner, in her private apartment with two or three ladies who were her most intimate friends.

'We were talking about M. de Nemours,' the Dauphine said when she saw her, 'and wondering at the change in him since his return from Brussels. Before he left, he had an infinite number of mistresses: it was even a weakness in him, since he treated those who deserved his attentions in the same way as those who did not. Since coming back, he pays no heed to any of them. There has never been so great a change, and I think it has even affected his humour, as he seems less carefree than previously.'

Mme de Clèves did not answer, but was ashamed to think that, before her mother had disabused her, she would have taken everything they were saying about the change in the prince as evidence of his love for her. She felt some annoyance at the Dauphine when she saw her hunting for reasons and showing surprise at something which, by all accounts, she ought to be able to explain better than anybody. She was unable to restrain herself from letting her know as much and, when the other ladies moved away, went across to her and whispered:

'Did you intend what you have just said for my ears as well, madame, and are you trying to conceal from me that you are the person who has inspired this change in M. de Nemours's behaviour?'

'You do me an injustice,' answered the Dauphine. 'You know that I hide nothing from you. It is true that, before going to Brussels, M. de Nemours intended, I think, to indicate to me that I was not displeasing to him. But, since his return, I cannot believe that he even remembers what he did, and I admit that I am curious to know what has altered him. It is unlikely that I shall not get to the truth of it,' she added. 'His close friend, the Vidame de Chartres, is in love with a woman over whom I have some influence and by those means I shall learn the reason for this change.'

The way in which the Dauphine spoke convinced Mme de Clèves and, despite herself, she felt calmer and better disposed than before.

When she returned to her mother's, she learned that her condition had worsened considerably since she had left. Her fever had mounted and rose during the next few days to indicate a serious illness. Mme de Clèves was extremely distressed and did not leave her mother's room. M. de Clèves also visited almost daily, both because he was concerned for Mme de Chartres and to prevent his wife lapsing into despair, as well as for the pleasure of seeing her, for his love had not diminished.

M. de Nemours, who had always had a great liking for him, continued to demonstrate it after his return from Brussels. During Mme de Chartres's illness, he several times managed to see Mme de Clèves on the pretext of visiting her husband or coming to take him out for a walk. He even looked for him at times when he knew he would not be there and, on the excuse of waiting for him, remained in Mme de Chartres's antechamber, where there were always several persons of quality. Mme de Clèves often came there and, though she was worried, seemed no less beautiful to M. de Nemours. He demonstrated his concern for her in her distress and spoke to her with such a tender and deferential air that she was easily convinced it was not the Dauphine whom he loved.

She could not help being disturbed at seeing him, yet took pleasure in seeing him. But when he was no longer to be seen, and when she considered that the delight she took in seeing him was the start of a passionate attachment, she almost thought she hated him for the pain that this idea gave her.

Mme de Chartres's condition deteriorated to the point where they began to despair for her life. She accepted what the doctors told her about the danger she was in with a courage worthy of her virtue and her piety. When they had left, she dismissed everyone and called for Mme de Clèves.

'My daughter, we must part,' she said, holding out her hand. 'My pain at having to leave you is intensified by the peril in which you stand and your need for my help. You are attracted to M. de Nemours – I don't ask you to admit it: I am not now in a state where I could make use of your sincerity to guide you. I noticed your liking for him a long time ago, but at first I did not want to mention it to you, for fear that I might make you aware of it yourself. Now you know it only too well. You are on the brink of the precipice: you will need to make an immense effort against your own inclinations to hold back. Think of your duty to your husband, think of your duty to yourself, and consider that you will lose the reputation you have gained and which I so much desired for you. Be strong and brave, my daughter; retire from the court, force your husband to take you away, do not be afraid that this course will be too harsh or too difficult, however much it appals you at first: in the long run, it will be easier than the unhappiness of an affair. If any arguments other than those of virtue and duty could persuade you to do as I ask, I should tell you that, were there a single thing that might disturb the bliss to which I look forward on leaving this world, it would be to see you fall as other women have done. But, if this misfortune is to occur, I die happy, since I shall not have to witness it.'

Mme de Clèves dissolved into tears on her mother's hand, which she was holding between her own, and Mme de Chartres was herself so moved that she said:

'Farewell, my daughter. Let us end this conversation, which is too affecting for us both, and remember, if you can, what I have just told you.'

As she said this, she turned away, asking her daughter to call her women, not wanting to listen to her or speak any further. Mme de Clèves left her mother's room in a state that can be imagined and Mme de Chartres thought only of preparing herself for death. She lingered for two days, during which she did not again want to see her daughter, the only thing on earth to which she felt any attachment.

Mme de Clèves was deeply distressed. Her husband did not leave her side and, as soon as Mme de Chartres was dead, took her to the country, to remove her from a place which could only intensify her suffering, the like of which has never been seen: though affection and gratitude played the greatest part in it, her awareness that she needed her mother to protect her against M. de Nemours was a major consideration. She was distressed at being left to herself at a time when she was so little in control of her feelings and when she would so much have wished for someone to sympathize with her and give her strength. M. de Clèves's treatment of her made her desire more earnestly than ever not to fail in her duty towards him. Thus she showed him more tenderness and affection than ever before; she did not want him to leave her and felt that, if she attached herself to him, he would protect her against M. de Nemours.

The latter came to visit M. de Clèves in the country. He also did his best to see Mme de Clèves, but she did not want to receive him and, fully aware that she would be unable not to find him attractive, had firmly resolved to avoid seeing him and to prevent any opportunity of doing so when it depended on her.

M. de Clèves went to Paris to attend court and promised his wife that he would only be away until the next day; however, he did not return until the day following that.

'I waited for you all yesterday,' Mme de Clèves said when he arrived, 'and I must reproach you for not coming back when you promised you would. You know that if I could feel any added grief in my present state, it would be at the death of Mme de Tournon, of which I learned this morning. I should have been moved by it even if I had not known her: the death of a woman so young and beautiful as her, in a mere two days, is always something to excite pity; but, in addition to that, she was one of the people whom I most liked in the world and who seemed as intelligent as she was good.'

'I was very sorry not to come back yesterday,' M. de Clèves replied. 'But my presence was so essential to comfort someone in distress that I could not leave him. As for Mme de Tournon, I advise you save your tears, if you are mourning a woman whom you believe to be full of common sense and worthy of your esteem.'

'You amaze me,' Mme de Clèves said. 'Several times I have heard you remark that there was no woman at court for whom you had more respect.'

'Yes, that is so,' he answered, 'but women are incomprehensible and, when I see all the rest, I am amazed at my good fortune in having you.'

'You admire me more than I deserve,' replied Mme de Clèves, sighing, 'and it is too soon to find me worthy of you. But please tell me what changed your mind about Mme de Tournon.'

'It changed a long time ago,' he said, 'since I learned that she was in love with the Comte de Sancerre and encouraged him to think that she might marry him.'

'I cannot believe,' Mme de Clèves interjected, 'that Mme de Tournon, in view of her extraordinary aversion to marriage after her husband's death, and her public declarations that she would never remarry, should have offered any hope to Sancerre.'

'If it had only been to him,' replied M. de Clèves, 'there would be no cause for surprise. What is truly astonishing is that she simultaneously offered the same to Estouteville; but let me tell you the full story.'

Book Two

———

'Sancerre, as you know, is one of my closest friends; yet, some two years ago, when he fell in love with Mme de Tournon, he took great care to keep it secret from me, as from everyone else. I had not the slightest suspicion. Mme de Tournon still seemed inconsolable after the death of her husband and lived in strict retirement. Sancerre's sister was almost the only person whom she visited, and it was at her house that he fell in love.

'One evening when a play was to be performed at the Louvre and the players were only waiting for the King and Mme de Valentinois to arrive, word was sent that she was ill and that the King would not attend after all. We immediately guessed that the "illness" was in reality a dispute between her and the King. We knew how jealous he had been of the Maréchal de Brissac during his stay at court, but the Maréchal had returned to Piedmont a few days before and we could not imagine the cause of the quarrel.

'While I was discussing it with Sancerre, M. d'Anville came into the theatre and whispered to me that the King was in a pitiful state of rage; that, a few days earlier, during a reconciliation with Mme de Valentinois over their quarrel about the Maréchal de Brissac, the King had given her a ring and begged her to wear it; that, while she was dressing to come to the play, he had noticed she did not have this ring and enquired the reason; that she seemed amazed at being without it and asked her women; but they, either through inadvertence or ignorance, replied that they had not seen it for four or five days.

'"That corresponded exactly to the time since the Maréchal de Brissac's departure," M. d'Anville continued, "so the King did not doubt that she had given the ring to him while they were taking leave of each other. The idea excited his jealousy (which was not fully allayed) to such an extent that he flew into an uncommon rage and soundly reprimanded her. He has just returned home in a state of great distress, but I am not certain whether this is due more to the idea of Mme de Valentinois giving up her ring, or to the fear of having displeased her by his anger."

'As soon as M. d'Anville had finished telling me this news, I went over to Sancerre to pass it on to him, as a secret that had just been imparted to me, forbidding him to speak about it.

'The next morning, I went quite early to my sister-in-law's and found Mme de Tournon at her bedside. She did not like Mme de Valentinois and knew very well that my sister-in-law felt the same. Sancerre had been to see Mme de Tournon on leaving the play and informed her of the King's dispute with the duchess, so Mme de Tournon had come to tell my sister-in-law, either without knowing, or without considering that I was the one who had told the story to her lover.

'As soon as I came into my sister-in-law's, she told Mme de Tournon that it was safe to pass on the story to me and, without waiting for Mme de Tournon's permission, recounted word for word everything that I had said to Sancerre the evening before. You can imagine my astonishment. I looked at Mme de Tournon, and thought she seemed embarrassed. Her embarrassment made me suspicious: I had spoken to no one apart from Sancerre and he had left me outside the theatre, without explanation. I also remembered how highly he had praised Mme de Tournon. All these things combined to open my eyes and I had no trouble in drawing the conclusion that he was romantically involved with her, and that he had been to see her after leaving me.

'I was so irritated to find out that he had been hiding this liaison from me, that I made several remarks to let Mme de

Tournon realize how indiscreet she had been. I handed her into her carriage and assured her, as I took my leave, that I envied the happiness of the person who had informed her of the quarrel between the King and Mme de Valentinois.

'I immediately set off to find Sancerre and reprimanded him, telling him that I knew of his attachment to Mme de Tournon, not saying how I had learned of it. He was forced to confess, so I told him what had given it away to me. He went on to tell me the details of their affair. He said that, even though he was the youngest in his family and so far from being able to aspire to such a good match, she was nonetheless determined to marry him. I suggested that he hurry her to the altar, since he could expect anything from a woman deceitful enough to have kept up a public face so distant from her true one. He replied that she had been genuinely distressed, but that her feeling for him had overcome her grief, and that she could not suddenly exhibit such a great change in her behaviour. He made several other excuses for her, which showed me how much he was in love, and assured me that he would obtain her consent to my knowing of his passion, since it was she herself, after all, who had informed me of it. He did in fact persuade her to do so, though with great difficulty, and from then on I was taken into their closest confidence.

'Never have I seen a woman more correct and pleasing in her behaviour towards her lover; however, I continued to be shocked by her pretence of still mourning her husband. Sancerre was so deeply in love and so pleased by her treatment of him that he scarcely dared press her closer to marriage, fearing she would believe he desired it more for her money than because he truly loved her. Despite this, he did raise the matter and she seemed determined to marry him; she even began to emerge from retirement and return to society. She visited my sister-in-law at times when part of the court was there. Sancerre seldom went, but those who did every evening often saw her and found her company delightful.

'Shortly after she had begun to leave her seclusion, Sancerre thought he noticed some cooling in her love for him. He mentioned it to me several times, though I could not see any grounds for concern. But, eventually, when he told me that instead of making arrangements for the marriage, she seemed to be putting it off, I started to think his suspicions might not be ill-founded. I told him he could expect Mme de Tournon's passion to cool after two years; that, even if undiminished, he should not complain if it were not strong enough to force her into marrying him; that this marriage would be extremely damaging to her in public opinion, because he was not a good enough match for her, and also because of the damage it would cause to her reputation; and, consequently, that the most he could expect was that she would not deceive him or give him any false hopes. I added that, if she did not have the strength of mind to marry him, or if she were to confess that she loved someone else, he should not complain or lose his temper, but show the same respect and gratitude towards her as before.

'"I am giving you the advice," I said, "that I should follow myself: for I set such high store by sincerity that I think if my mistress or even my wife were to tell me she was attracted to someone else, I should be upset, but not bitter. I should cease to behave as a lover or a husband, so that I could offer her my advice and sympathy."'

These words made Mme de Clèves blush: she saw some reference in them to her own situation, and was so surprised and confused, that it was some time before she could recover her composure.

'Sancerre spoke to Mme de Tournon,' M. de Clèves continued, 'and told her everything that I had advised; but she reassured him so scrupulously and seemed so offended by his suspicions that she entirely removed them. Yet she asked to delay their marriage until after a fairly long journey that he was to make; but she behaved so properly until his departure and appeared so grieved by it that, like him, I believed she truly loved him. He set out some three months ago. During his absence I saw little of Mme de Tournon: you have taken up all my time and all I knew was that he was shortly due to return.

'The day before yesterday, on my arrival in Paris, I learned that she was dead. I sent to enquire at his house to know whether there was any news of him. I was informed that he had come back on the previous day, the very day of Mme de Tournon's death. I went instantly to see him, easily anticipating his state of mind, but his distress was beyond anything I had imagined.

'I have never seen such heartfelt suffering. He at once embraced me, bursting into tears: "I shall see her no more," he said, "I shall see her no more, she is dead! I was not worthy of her, but I shall soon follow her!"

'After this, he said nothing; then, from time to time, repeating "she is dead, I shall see her no more!", he resumed his wailing and his tears, and continued to behave like a man who had lost his senses. He told me that he had received few letters from her while he was away, but he was not surprised at this, since he knew her and was aware that she felt uneasy at entrusting her letters to the courier. He had no doubt that she would have married him on his return, and considered her the most adorable and loyal person that ever lived. He believed himself to have been tenderly loved and was losing her at the very moment when he expected to be united with her for ever. All these thoughts plunged him into a violent distress that totally prostrated him. I admit that I could not help being moved by it myself.

'However, I was obliged to leave him to attend the King, but promised to return shortly. So I did, and have never been more astonished than at the change I found in him from when I had left. He was on his feet, in his room, with a frantic expression, walking, then stopping, as if he was out of his mind. "Come in, come in," he said, "come and see the most despairing of men, a thousand times more miserable than before: for I have just learned something about Mme de Tournon that is worse than her death."

'I thought that grief had completely deranged him, not

being able to imagine that there was anything worse than the death of a beloved mistress by whom one was loved in turn. I told him that so long as there were some bounds to his sorrow, I could applaud it and sympathize; but that I should have no sympathy were he to give in to despair and abandon all reason.

'"I should be only too happy to lose it, and life as well," he exclaimed. "Mme de Tournon was unfaithful to me, and I have learned of her infidelity and treachery the very day after her death, at a moment when my soul was utterly imbued with the deepest pain and most tender passion ever felt by man: at a time when my heart had embraced the image of her as the ultimate in perfection and the most perfect in her conduct towards me, I find that I was mistaken and that she does not deserve my tears; yet I endure the same grief at her death as if she had been faithful to me and suffer her infidelity as if she were still alive. Had I discovered this change in her before her death, I should have been filled with jealousy, fury and anger, inuring me in some way to the sorrow of her loss; but I am now in a state where I can neither be consoled, nor hate her."

'You may imagine my surprise: I asked Sancerre how he could substantiate any of this. He told me that a short while after I had left his room, Estouteville, a close friend (who, despite that, knew nothing of his love for Mme de Tournon) arrived to visit him. As soon as he sat down, he started to weep and begged Sancerre to forgive him for having concealed what he was about to disclose; he appealed for sympathy: he said he had come to open his heart; and that he saw before him the man who, of all men, was most deeply grieved by the death of Mme de Tournon.

'"That name," Sancerre went on, "startled me so much that my first impulse was to remark that I was still more deeply grieved than he was, but I could not find the strength to speak; so he continued, saying that he had been in love with her for six months; that he had always wanted to inform me of it, but that she strictly forbade him, in such emphatic terms that he dared not disobey; that her feeling for him had arisen almost at the same time as his for her, but they had concealed their love from everybody: he had never visited her publicly; that it had been his joy to console her for the death of her husband; and, finally, at the time of her death, he was to marry her; but this marriage, in reality the consequence of their love, was to seem the result of duty and obedience, since she had persuaded her father to order her to marry him, to avoid being accused of too sudden a change of heart, after she had been so firmly set against remarriage."

'"While Estouteville was telling me this," Sancerre went on, "I believed him, because his account seemed plausible; and the time when he said he had first fallen in love with Mme de Tournon was the very time when her feelings towards me appeared to have changed; but the moment after, I thought he must be lying or imagining things. I was about to say as much, then felt the need to be clear in my mind and questioned him, implying a doubt. In the end I went so far in trying to gain evidence of my misfortune that he asked if I knew Mme de Tournon's handwriting. He brought out four of her letters and her portrait, and put them on the bed. At this moment, my brother came in. Estouteville's face was so stained with tears that he had to retire, to avoid being seen. He said that he would come back in the evening to retrieve what he had left, and I asked my brother to go, on the grounds that I was feeling unwell, but in fact because I was impatient to see the letters that Estouteville had left, hoping to find something in them to contradict what he had said. Instead, what did I find? Such tenderness, such vows, such promises to marry him! What letters they were: she had never written any like them to me."

'"So," he continued, "I am simultaneously feeling the pain of her death and the pain of her unfaithfulness; and while these two types of pain have often been compared, they have never previously been felt by one person at one time. To my shame, I admit that I am still suffering her loss more than her change of heart: I cannot consider her so guilty that I would wish her dead. If she were alive, I should have the pleasure of blaming her and be avenged by making her acknowledge the wrong she has done me. But I shall see her no more," he repeated, "I shall see her no more! There is the greatest misfortune of all. I wish I could give my own life to restore hers – but what a wish! If she did return, she would live only for Estouteville. How happy I was yesterday!" he exclaimed. "How happy! I was the most miserable man in the world, but my grief was reasoned and I found some comfort in the idea that I would never be consoled. Today, I can justify nothing that I feel. I am paying the same debt of sorrow to the feelings she pretended for me, as I thought I owed to an unfeigned attachment. I can neither hate her memory, nor love it; I can neither find consolation, nor mourn."

'"At the very least," he said, abruptly turning towards me, "make sure, I beg you, that I never see Estouteville again: his very name appals me. I know quite well I have no reason to blame him: it was my own fault for concealing my love for Mme de Tournon; had he known of it, he would perhaps not have become attached to her, and she would not have been unfaithful to me. He came to me to confide his sorrow, and I grieve for him. Ah, rightly so," he cried, "for he loved Mme de Tournon, was loved by her and will never see her again; yet I know that I cannot prevent myself from hating him. So, once again, I implore you to contrive that I may not see him."

'At this, Sancerre began to weep again, to mourn Mme de Tournon, to address her, saying the most affectionate things imaginable; then he turned to anger, wailing, reproaches and curses against her. Seeing him in such an uncontrollable state, I realized that I needed help to calm his mind. I sent for his brother, whom I had just left at the King's, spoke to him in the outer room before he entered and described Sancerre's condition. We gave orders to prevent him seeing Estouteville and spent part of the night attempting to restore him to a more reasonable frame of mind. But this morning, I found him more distressed than ever. His brother stayed with him and I have returned to your side.'

'No one could be more surprised than I am,' Mme de Clèves said at this point. 'I considered Mme de Tournon incapable of either love or deceit.'

'Artifice and dissimulation,' M. de Clèves continued, 'have never been taken further than by her. Observe that when Sancerre believed her feelings had changed towards him, this was really the case and she had begun to love Estouteville. She told him that he was consoling her for her husband's death, and that he was the cause of her return to society; yet Sancerre thought it was because we had decided that she should not remain in deep mourning. She explained to Estouteville that he must keep their understanding a secret and that she must seem to be forced to marry him in accordance with her father's wishes, through concern for her reputation; yet it was so that she could abandon Sancerre without giving him grounds to complain. I must go back,' M. de Clèves went on, 'and see this unfortunate man; and I think that you too must return to Paris. It is time that you met people and received all those many, unavoidable visits of condolence.'

Mme de Clèves agreed and left the next day. She was now easier in her mind about M. de Nemours: everything that Mme de Chartres had said on her deathbed, as well as the pain of losing her, had put her feelings into abeyance, and this made her think that they had been altogether erased.

On the evening of her arrival, the Dauphine came to see her and, after expressing condolences for her loss, told her that, to distract her from these sad thoughts, she would like to inform her of everything that happened at court during her absence; and she continued with a detailed account.

'But the thing I most want to tell you,' she went on, 'is that it is now established that M. de Nemours is passionately in love. But not only has he withheld the secret from his most intimate friends, they cannot even guess who may be the woman he loves. Yet this passion is strong enough to make him neglect or, more precisely, give up his hopes of a crown.'

The Dauphine then told her everything that had happened with regard to the English throne, continuing:

'All this I learned from M. d'Anville, who told me this morning that the King sent for M. de Nemours yesterday evening, on receipt of letters from Lignerolles, begging permission to return and telling the King that he can no longer defend M. de Nemours's dilatoriness to the English Queen: she is starting to be offended by it, since, even though she had given no definite response, she had said enough for him to venture on the journey. The King read this letter to M. de Nemours and he, instead of replying seriously as he had at the start, only laughed, joked and made fun of Lignerolles's expectations. He said that he would be condemned as rash by the whole of Europe if he were to risk going to England as someone who pretended to the Queen's hand, unless he were assured of success, adding, "I also think I should be wasting my time on this journey now, when the King of Spain is doing his utmost to marry this Queen. He is perhaps not a rival much to be feared in love, but I would suggest that when it comes to marriage, Your Majesty would not advise me to cross swords with him." "I should advise you to do so in this instance," the King replied. "But you will have no quarrel with him, for I know he has other ideas; and, even if he did not, Queen Mary suffered too much from the Spanish yoke for anyone to believe that her sister would wish to put it on her own shoulders, or would be dazzled by the brilliance of so many united crowns." "If she is not dazzled," M. de Nemours answered, "then apparently she would like to find happiness in love. Some years ago, she loved Lord Courtenay: he was also loved by Queen Mary, who would have married him with the approval of the whole country, had she not known that the youth and beauty of her sister Elizabeth touched him more deeply than hope of the crown. Your Majesty knows that her passionate jealousy on this score induced her to put them both in prison, then to exile Lord Courtenay and, finally, decided her to marry the King of Spain. Now that Elizabeth is on the throne, I am sure she will soon remember that nobleman, and choose one she has already loved, who deserves her and has suffered so much for her, rather than another whom she has never seen."

' "I would agree," replied the King, "if Courtenay were still alive; but a few days ago I learned of his death in exile in Padua. I can see," he added, on leaving M. de Nemours, "that your marriage will have to be concluded by proxy as one would with the Dauphin's, sending ambassadors to marry the English Queen."

'M. d'Anville and the Vidame, who were present with M. de Nemours, are convinced that this same overwhelming passion has distracted him from so great an endeavour. The Vidame, who is closer to him than anybody, told Mme de Martigues that he is altered beyond recognition. What is still more surprising is that no one has observed any relationship or any particular times at which he escapes notice, so that the Vidame does not think he has an understanding with the person he loves: if M. de Nemours is unrecognizable, it is because he appears to be in love with a woman who does not love him in return.'

What torment the Dauphine's words were for Mme de Clèves! How could she fail to recognize herself in this unknown person, or to be filled with gratitude and affection on learning, from an unimpeachable source, that the duke, who already had a place in her heart, was hiding his passion from everyone and neglecting the opportunity of gaining a throne, for love of her? So her feelings and agitation of mind cannot be described. Had the Dauphine looked at her carefully, she would easily have seen that her words were not a matter of indifference to Mme de Clèves; but, having no suspicion of the truth, she went on regardless:

'As I mentioned, I had all this from M. d'Anville, though he thinks that I know more about it than he does: he has such a high opinion of my charms that he is convinced I am the only person who could bring about such a change in M. de Nemours.'

These last words of the Dauphine's caused Mme de Clèves to feel a different kind of agitation from the one she had experienced a few moments before.

'I could well agree with M. d'Anville,' she replied. 'It seems more than likely, madame, that it would take no less a princess than yourself to make him despise the Queen of England.'

'I should admit it if I knew it,' retorted the Dauphine, 'and I should know it if it were true. That sort of passion does not escape those who inspire it: they are the first to notice. M. de Nemours never showed more than a slight partiality towards me, yet there is such a great difference between his manner when he was with me previously and his manner now that I can assure you it is not I who am the cause of his indifference to the English throne.'

'But I am forgetting the time,' the Dauphine added. 'I ought to go and see Madame. You know that the peace treaty has almost been signed: what you do not know is that the King of Spain was unwilling to accept a single article except on condition that he might be allowed to marry the princess[14] himself, in place of his son Don Carlos. The King was very loath to agree, but at last did so, and is just about to announce the news to Madame. I believe that she will be inconsolable: the prospect of marrying a man of the Spanish King's age and character is hardly agreeable, especially to her, when she possesses all the joy of youth, as well as beauty, and was expecting to marry a young prince to whom she felt attracted even without having met him. I do not know if the King will find her submissive as he might wish: he has asked me to see her, because he knows that she loves me and thinks I may have some influence with her. After that, I have a quite different call to make: I shall go and celebrate with Madame, the King's sister. Everything is settled for her to marry M. de Savoie and he will arrive shortly. Never has anyone of her age been so delighted to marry. The court will be thronged with more and more beautiful people than have ever been seen and, despite your loss, you must come to help us demonstrate to the foreign guests that we possess the finest beauties.'

At this, the Dauphine left Mme de Clèves, and the next day Madame's marriage was publicly announced. On the

days that followed, the King and the Queens came to visit
Mme de Clèves. M. de Nemours, who had been waiting with
the utmost impatience for her return and who was most
anxious to find an opportunity of speaking to her alone,
waited before going to her house for the time when everyone
was retiring and when it seemed unlikely that anyone else
would arrive. His plan was successful and he entered just as
the last visitors were taking their leave.

Mme de Clèves was on her bed. It was a warm day and the
sight of M. de Nemours heightened her colour in a way that
did not detract from her beauty. He sat opposite her, with
the misgivings and diffidence that are born of true passion.
For a time, he could say nothing. Mme de Clèves was equally
speechless, so that there was a rather long silence between
them. Finally, M. de Nemours broke it, to offer his condolences in her sorrow. Mme de Clèves, very pleased to continue
the conversation along these lines, spoke for quite a time
about her loss and finally said that, even when time had
assuaged the violence of her suffering, she would have been
so deeply affected by it that her temperament would have
changed.

'Great suffering and violent passion,' M. de Nemours interjected, 'produce great alteration in the mind. In my own
case, I cannot recognize myself since my return from Flanders. Many people have remarked on the change in me, and
the Dauphine herself mentioned it to me only yesterday.'

'It is true,' said Mme de Clèves, 'that she has noticed it and
I believe I heard her say something on the matter.'

'I am not sorry, madame, that she should have observed
it,' replied M. de Nemours, 'but I wish she were not alone in
having done so. There are those to whom we dare give no
sign of the love that we feel for them, except in things that do
not touch them directly; and, though one dares not show
them that they are loved, one would at least like them to see
that one does not wish to be loved by anyone else. One
would hope them to know that there is no beauty, whatever
her rank in society, whom one would not look upon with

indifference, and that there is no crown that one would wish to purchase at the price of not seeing them again. Ordinarily,' he went on, 'women assess the extent of our feeling for them by our persistence in trying to please them and in seeking them out. But that requires little effort, provided they are personable; the real test is not to give way to the pleasure of being with them; it lies in avoiding them, for fear of revealing to others, and almost to themselves, the feeling that we have for them. And what still more clearly distinguishes true devotion is to become entirely the opposite of what one has been, and to abandon ambition and pleasure, when one's whole life has been devoted to those things.'

Mme de Clèves had no difficulty in understanding that this speech was referring to her. It occurred to her that she ought to reply and not to endure it. It occurred to her also that she should not understand or give any sign that she applied what he said to herself. She felt she should speak and thought she should say nothing. M. de Nemours's words almost equally pleased and offended her; they confirmed all that the Dauphine had led her to think; she found something in them that was on the one hand gallant and respectful, yet on the other forward and only too plain. Her partiality for the prince created an unease in her that she could not control. The most obscure discourse of an attractive man is more disturbing than an open declaration of love from one who is not. So she gave no reply, and M. de Nemours might have noticed her silence – and perhaps interpreted it in his favour – had the arrival of M. de Clèves not put an end to the conversation and to his visit.

He had come to give his wife news of Sancerre, though she was not very curious to know the end of his story. She was so preoccupied with what had just taken place that she could hardly conceal the fact that her mind was elsewhere. When she was free to pursue her own thoughts, she realized full well that she had been wrong to think she no longer felt anything but indifference towards M. de Nemours. His speech had made as deep an impression as ever he could have wished

and entirely convinced her of his love. His actions corresponded too well with his words for there to be any doubt in
the princess's mind. She no longer deluded herself with the
hope that she could avoid loving him; she only considered
how to ensure that he should never guess her feelings. It was
a hard task: she already knew how hard; she knew that the
only road to success lay in avoiding his presence; and, since
her mourning was a reason for her to be more retiring than
usual, she used this excuse to stop going to places where he
might see her. She was plunged into deep sadness: her
mother's death seemed the cause and no one looked for any
other.

M. de Nemours was desperate at hardly seeing her any
more and, knowing that he would not find her at those
assemblies or entertainments attended by the whole court, he
could not bring himself to take part. Instead, he pretended to
have a great passion for hunting and went out to hunt on the
days when there were receptions at the Queens' houses. A
slight illness was his pretext for a long stay at home and for
not going to all the places where he realized Mme de Clèves
would not be.

M. de Clèves fell ill at around the same time. Mme de
Clèves did not leave his room during his illness; but, when he
was better, when he started to receive visitors, among them
M. de Nemours who, on the excuse of his being still weak,
spent the greater part of the day there, she found that she
could not remain with him; yet she could not bring herself to
go out the first times that he came. It had been too long since
she had seen him for her to find the strength not to see him.
The prince managed to let her know, in words that appeared
merely commonplace (but that she understood even so, because they related to what he had said on his visit to her),
that he went hunting so that he could be alone with his
thoughts, and that he did not go to any public assembly
because she was not there.

At last, she carried out her resolve to leave her husband's
room when he came, though it meant the most painful struggle

with herself. The prince quite understood that she was fleeing from him, and was deeply affected.

At first, M. de Clèves took no notice of his wife's behaviour; but at length he observed that she did not want to stay in his room when other people were there. He mentioned it to her, and she replied that she did not think it proper that she should spend every evening with all the youngest members of the court; that she begged him to see fit that she should have a more retiring life than before; that morality and the presence of her mother had made a lot of things acceptable that could not be justified in a woman of her age.

M. de Clèves, who was naturally disposed to kindness and indulgence as far as his wife was concerned, showed none on this occasion and told her that he absolutely opposed any change in her conduct. She was on the point of telling him that it was publicly rumoured M. de Nemours was in love with her, but she did not have the courage to utter his name. She also felt ashamed at wishing to suggest what was not the true reason, and to conceal the truth from a man who held her in such high regard.

A few days later, the King was with the Queen at the time when she received her friends: they were speaking about horoscopes and predictions. Opinion was divided as to how far these could be relied on. The Queen had great faith in them: she argued that, after so many things had been predicted then seen to take place, it was impossible not to believe that this was something of a precise science. Others argued that, in the vast number of predictions made, the few that proved to be true merely demonstrated that it was only an effect of chance.

'I used at one time to be very curious about the future,' the King said. 'But I have been told so many things that are false or implausible that I have become convinced nothing certain can be known. A few years ago, a man came here who had a great reputation for astrology.[15] Everyone went to see him, I with the rest, but not revealing who I was. I took M. de Guise and M. d'Escars, and let them go in before me.

Nonetheless, the astrologer addressed himself firstly to me, as if he judged me to have precedence; perhaps he had recognized me; yet, if he did, he told me something quite inappropriate. He predicted I should be killed in a duel. Then he told M. de Guise that he would be killed from behind and M. d'Escars that he would have his skull broken by a kick from a horse. M. de Guise was almost offended by his prediction, as if being accused of running away at some time. D'Escars was scarcely more pleased at learning he would die from such an unfortunate accident. In the end we all came away very discontented with the astrologer. I do not know what will happen to M. de Guise or M. d'Escars, but there seems little likelihood that I shall be killed in a duel. The King of Spain and I have just made peace; and, even if that were not so, I doubt very much if we should have fought in a duel, or that I should challenge him as the king, my father, challenged Charles V.'

After the misfortune that the King said had been predicted for him, those who supported astrology gave in and agreed that one should put no trust in it.

'As for me,' said M. de Nemours, 'I am the person in the world who should trust it the least'; and, turning to Mme de Clèves, who was sitting next to him, whispered: 'It has been foretold that I shall be made happy through the favours of the person in the world for whom I shall have the most overwhelming and respectful passion. It is for you to judge, madame, whether I should believe in predictions.'

The Dauphine, assuming from what M. de Nemours had said aloud, that he was whispering some false prediction he had been given, asked the prince what he was saying to Mme de Clèves. If he had had less presence of mind, he would have been embarrassed by the question. But, with no hesitation, he replied:

'I was remarking, madame, that it was foretold me I should attain a much greater fortune than I could ever have dared aspire to.'

'If that is the only prediction you have been given,'

answered the Dauphine, thinking of the English business, 'I should not advise you to disparage astrology: you might well find reason to support it.'

Mme de Clèves knew just what the Dauphine meant, but she also realized that the good fortune M. de Nemours was speaking about was not that of becoming King of England.

Since it was now quite some time since her mother's death, she had to start appearing in public and resume her accustomed duties at court. She saw M. de Nemours at the Dauphine's; she saw him at the house of M. de Clèves, where he often came with other noblemen of his own age, so as not to attract notice; but she no longer saw him without feeling an emotion that he was easily able to detect.

However hard she tried to avoid catching his eye or to speak to him less than to others, her first impulse betrayed her, allowing the prince to conclude that she was not indifferent to him. A less perceptive man might not have realized this, but he had already been loved so many times that he could hardly remain unaware when a woman was in love with him. He observed, too, that he had a rival in the Chevalier de Guise, who equally well knew that M. de Nemours was his rival. The Chevalier was the only man at court who could have uncovered the truth: having himself a stake in the matter, he saw more clearly than anyone else, and this knowledge of their feelings created a bitterness between them that emerged at every point, though without breaking into an open quarrel; but they were at odds over everything. In tilting at rings, in tournaments or affrays, and in every diversion that entertained the King, they were always on opposite sides, and their rivalry was so great that it could not be disguised.

Mme de Clèves often considered the business with England: she thought that M. de Nemours would not hold out against the King's advice and the urging of Lignerolles. She was sorry to note that the latter had still not returned and she waited impatiently for him to do so. If she had given in to impulse, she would have discovered as much as she could about the matter; but the same feeling that made her curious obliged her to hide her curiosity and she only enquired about Queen Elizabeth's appearance, mind and character. A portrait of the Queen was brought to the King; she considered it more beautiful than she would have wished, and could not restrain herself from describing it as flattering.

'I think not,' replied the Dauphine, who was there. 'The Queen has a reputation for beauty and a quite exceptional mind: I might say that all my life she has been held up to me as an example. She must be a most attractive person if she resembles her mother, Anne Boleyn: there was never any woman who possessed such charm and allure, both in her person and in her character. I have heard that there was something vivacious and uncommon about her face, and that she had a beauty quite different from that of other English women.'

'I think it has also been said,' Mme de Clèves continued, 'that she was born in France.'

'Those who believed that were wrong,' the Dauphine answered, 'and I shall briefly tell you her story.

'She came from a good English family. Henry VIII had been in love with both her sister and her mother, and it was even suspected that she might be his daughter. She came here with the sister of Henry VII, who married King Louis XII. This princess was young and loved gallantry, so she found it very hard to leave the French court after her husband's death; but Anne Boleyn, whose temperament was similar to her mistress's, could not tear herself away. The late King was in love with her, and she remained as lady-in-waiting to Queen Claude. When the Queen died, the King's sister took her into her household: this was Mme Marguerite,[16] Duchesse d'Alençon and later Queen of Navarre, whose stories you have read; and, under her influence, Anne was tainted with the new religion. She subsequently returned to England, where she won every heart: she had those French manners that delight all nations; she sang well and danced superbly; she was appointed lady-in-waiting to Queen Katharine, and King Henry VIII fell hopelessly in love with her.

'Cardinal Wolsey, his favourite and first minister, had aspired to become Pope, but his ambitions were not supported by the Holy Roman Emperor; so Wolsey, displeased with the Emperor, decided to have his revenge by arranging for his master, the King, to be united with the French royal family. He insinuated to Henry VIII that his marriage to the Emperor's aunt was null and void, and suggested he marry the Duchesse d'Alençon, whose husband had just died. Anne Boleyn was ambitious, and considered this divorce as a path that might lead her to the throne. She started to put ideas into the English King's mind about the Lutheran faith and pledged our own late King to support Henry's divorce in Rome, on the expectation of his marriage to Mme d'Alençon. Cardinal Wolsey had himself sent to France on another pretext, in order to deal with this; but his master could not even bear to hear the matter proposed and sent him an order, to Calais, not to mention the marriage.

'On his return from France, Cardinal Wolsey was received with the same ceremony as that accorded to the King himself: never has any favourite's pride and vanity soared to such heights. He negotiated a meeting between the two Kings, which took place in Boulogne. François I offered his hand to Henry VIII, who would not take it. Turn by turn, they entertained each other with extraordinary splendour, each giving the other clothes like the ones he had had made for himself. I remember hearing that those the late King sent to the King of England were of crimson satin, brocaded in a triangular pattern, with pearls and diamonds, and the robe in white velvet embroidered in gold. After spending some days in Boulogne, they returned to Calais. Anne Boleyn was accommodated by King Henry with the suite of a Queen, and François I accorded her the same presents and honours as if she had been one. Finally, having loved her for nine years, Henry married her without waiting for the dissolution of his first marriage, which he had long before requested from Rome. The Pope was over-hasty in excommunicating him, and Henry was so incensed that he declared himself head of

the Church and took all England after him into the unfortunate changes that you now see.

'Anne Boleyn did not long enjoy her glory: when the death
of Katharine of Aragon had made her feel more secure in it,
one day as she was with the whole court, watching her brother
Lord Rochford tilting at rings, the King was stricken with
such jealousy that he abruptly left the scene, returned to
London and gave orders to arrest the Queen, with Lord
Rochford and several others whom he suspected of being her
lovers or confidants. Though this jealousy seemed to have
arisen in a moment, the seeds of it had been planted some
time earlier by Lady Rochford, who could not abide her
husband's close association with the Queen and so suggested
to the King that their intimacy was an illicit one. Hence the
King, who was in any case in love with Jane Seymour,
thought only how he might rid himself of Anne. In less than
three weeks, he brought her to trial beside her brother, then
had them both beheaded, and married Jane Seymour. He
subsequently took several wives, whom he either divorced or
had put to death, among them Katharine Howard, who was
Lady Rochford's confidante and was executed beside her.
Lady Rochford was thus punished for the crime of which she
had accused Anne Boleyn, and Henry VIII died, having
become enormously fat.'

All the ladies present during the Dauphine's account,
thanked her for having so well instructed them on the English
court, including Mme de Clèves, who could not refrain from
asking several further questions about Queen Elizabeth.

The Dauphine had miniatures painted of all the finest ladies
in court, to send them to her mother, the Queen. On the day
when that of Mme de Clèves was to be completed, the Dauphine went to spend the afternoon with her. M. de Nemours
made sure to be there: he did not let slip any opportunity to
see Mme de Clèves, though without appearing to make a
point of it. That day, she was so beautiful that, if he had not
already fallen in love with her, he would have done so then.
Yet he did not dare keep his eyes on her while she was being

painted and was afraid that the pleasure he had in watching her might be too plain.

The Dauphine asked M. de Clèves to let her see a little portrait he had of his wife, so that she could compare it with the one that was then being finished. Everyone gave an opinion on each of them, and Mme de Clèves asked the painter to make an adjustment to the hair on the one that had just been brought. The painter, to oblige her, took the miniature out of its box and, after working on it, replaced it on the table.

For a long time, M. de Nemours had wanted a portrait of Mme de Clèves. When he saw the one that belonged to M. de Clèves, he could not resist the temptation to purloin it from a husband whom he believed to be tenderly loved; and he thought that, among so many people present in one place, he would be under no more suspicion than anyone else.

The Dauphine was sitting on the bed, quietly speaking to Mme de Clèves who was standing in front of her. Through one of the curtains, which was only partly closed, Mme de Clèves noticed M. de Nemours with his back to the table at the foot of the bed, and observed that, without turning round, he adroitly removed something from it. She guessed at once that this was her portrait, and was so agitated that the Dauphine noticed she was not listening and asked her aloud what she was looking at. M. de Nemours, hearing this, turned and caught Mme de Clèves still staring at him, considering it quite probable she had seen what he had just done.

Mme de Clèves was not a little embarrassed. Normally, she should have asked him to return her portrait; but if she were to do so publicly, this would inform everybody of the prince's feelings for her; and to do it in private would mean virtually demanding that he should declare his love. At last, she decided that it was better to leave him the portrait; and she was happy to accord him a favour that it was possible for her to grant without his even knowing that she had done so. M. de Nemours, who noticed her confusion and guessed that he was its cause, came over to her and whispered:

'If you saw what I was so bold as to do, madame, be good

enough to let me think that you know nothing of it: I dare not ask more of you in the matter.'

With these words, he left and did not wait for her answer.

The Dauphine went out to walk, accompanied by all the ladies, while M. de Nemours returned home and remained indoors, not trusting himself in company to contain his joy at having a portrait of Mme de Clèves. He experienced the most pleasurable feelings that love can bestow: he loved the most admirable person at court; and he was winning her love in spite of herself, and observed, in her every action, that kind of confusion and perplexity that love causes in the innocence of early youth.

That evening, they looked everywhere for the portrait and, as they found the box where it ought to be, no one suspected that it could have been stolen: they thought it must have fallen off the table by accident. M. de Clèves was upset by the loss and, after another fruitless search had been made, said to his wife (though in tones that showed he did not believe it) that she must have a secret lover to whom she had given the portrait, or who had taken it, and that only a lover would have been satisfied at having the painting without the box.

Although these words were spoken in jest, they made a strong impression on Mme de Clèves. She had a feeling of guilt: she considered the force of her desire for M. de Nemours; she found that she was no longer in command of her voice or her expression; she remembered that Lignerolles had returned; that she was not worried any longer about the English business; that she had no further suspicions about the Dauphine; and finally that no defence was left to her, but that her only means of security was to go away. Yet, since she did not have the strength to do that, she found herself in dire straits, ready to fall into what seemed the greatest of misfortunes, which was to make M. de Nemours aware that she liked him. She remembered everything that Mme de Chartres had told her on her deathbed and her advice to adopt any course, however difficult, rather than to become enmeshed in an affair. She recalled what M. de Clèves had said about sincerity when speaking of Mme de Tournon; and she thought that she should admit her feeling for M. de Nemours to him. For a long time, she turned this idea over in her mind; and afterwards was amazed at even having considered it, decided it was madness, and returned to a state of indecision about the right course to take.

The peace treaty had been signed and, with great reluctance, Mme Elisabeth decided to obey her father, the King. The Duc d'Albe had been appointed to come and marry her as proxy for the Catholic King, and would soon arrive. The Duc de Savoie was also expected as husband for Madame, the King's sister, and the marriages would take place at the same time. The King's only consideration was to ensure that the weddings should be celebrated in such a way as to win renown for the brilliance and accomplishment of his court. He heard proposals for the finest plays and ballets that could be produced, but considered such entertainments too modest and asked for something that would make more of a show. He decided to hold a tournament, at which the foreign guests would be welcomed and which the people could watch. All the nobility and the young lords were delighted by the King's plan, particularly the Duc de Ferrare, M. de Guise and M. de Nemours, who were more skilled than any at this form of display. The King chose them to stand beside himself, as the four champions at the lists.

It was published throughout the kingdom that, in the City of Paris, on the fifteenth day of June, the joust would be opened by his Most Christian Majesty[17] and by the princes Alphonse d'Este, Duc de Ferrare; François de Lorraine, Duc de Guise; and Jacques de Savoie, Duc de Nemours; and that it would be held against all comers, the first combat to be on horseback in the lists, in double armour, four courses of the lance and one for the ladies; the second combat, with swords, singly or two against two, as the masters of the field should elect; the third combat on foot, three thrusts of the pike and six of the sword. That the champions should supply lances, swords and pikes, the choice being with the challengers; that if any combatant in the charge were to wound a horse, he should be put out of the lists; that there should be four masters of the field to issue commands, those of the combatants who had broken the most weapons and fought best having a reward at the discretion of the judges; that all participants, whether French or foreign, should be required to come before the shields hanging at the perron at the far end of the lists and touch one or several, as they wished; that they would find there a herald who would enrol them according to their rank and the shields they had touched; that the combatants should be required to have their shields, with their coats of arms, brought by a squire to be hung at the perron for three days before the start of the tournament, failing which they would not be admitted without leave from the champions.

Great lists were set up close to the Bastille, extending from the Château de Tournelles, across the rue Saint-Antoine, as far as the royal stables. On each side there was scaffolding and banked seating with covered boxes to form a sort of gallery which was very fine to look at and could accommodate an infinite number of people. Not one of the princes and lords could think of anything but to order all that was necessary for them to appear to the best advantage and to include, in their ciphers and devices, some gallantry appropriate to the women they loved.

A few days before the arrival of the Duc d'Albe, the King had a game of tennis with M. de Nemours, the Duc de Guise and the Vidame de Chartres. The Queens came to see them play, followed by all the ladies and, among these, Mme de Clèves. When the game was done, as everyone was leaving the court, Chastelart went up to the Reine Dauphine and told her that, by chance, he had come into possession of a love letter that had fallen out of M. de Nemours's pocket. The Dauphine, ever curious to know anything at all about the prince, told Chastelart to give it to her. She took it and followed the Queen, her mother-in-law, who had come with the King to inspect work on the lists. When they had been there for a little while, the King asked for some horses that he had had brought a short time before. Though they were not yet broken in, he wanted to ride them and gave some to all those who had followed him. The King and M. de Nemours found themselves on the most fiery: the two horses tried to charge one another. M. de Nemours, fearful that the King might be hurt, backed off sharply and turned his horse against a pillar of the exercise area, with such force that it shook. People ran across, thinking he had sustained a considerable injury. Mme de Clèves, more than anyone, thought him seriously hurt. Because of her feeling for the prince she experienced an anxiety and distress that she did not think to hide. She went up to him with the Queens, with a look of such concern that even someone less directly involved than the Chevalier de Guise would have seen it: so he noticed it easily and gave far more attention to the state of Mme de Clèves than to that of M. de Nemours. The blow that the prince had given himself stunned him to such an extent that he remained for some time with his head resting on those who were supporting him. When he looked up, the first thing he saw was Mme de Clèves, and he recognized the sympathy that she felt for him in her expression, which he returned in a way that allowed her to see how deeply he was touched by it. Then he thanked the Queens for the kindness they showed him and offered them his excuses for appearing in such a state in front of them. The King ordered him to go and rest.

Mme de Clèves, recovering from her fright, soon reflected on the signs of it that she must have given. The Chevalier de Guise did not long leave her to hope that it had gone unobserved. He offered her his hand to conduct her from the lists.

'I am more to be pitied than M. de Nemours, madame,' he said. 'Forgive me, if I put aside the deep respect that I have always had for you and disclose the extent of my pain at what I have just witnessed: this is the first time that I have been bold enough to speak to you, and it will be the last.

Death, or at least an everlasting exile, will remove me from a place in which I can no longer live, since I have just lost the melancholy consolation of believing that all those who dare to look upon you are as unfortunate as I am.'

Mme de Clèves answered with only a few disjointed words, as if she had not understood the implications of what the Chevalier de Guise was saying. In other circumstances, she would have been offended at him for speaking about his feelings for her; but at that moment, she experienced only the confusion of realizing that he had noticed hers for M. de Nemours. The Chevalier de Guise was certain of it, and so stricken with anguish that he resolved from that day onward never to hope that he might be loved by Mme de Clèves. But in order to renounce this project, that had seemed to him so difficult and so glorious, he needed to have another great enterprise to occupy him. He decided to take Rhodes[18] – an idea he already had in mind – and when death removed him from the world in the flower of youth, at a moment when he had gained the reputation of one of the greatest princes of his time, he expressed only one regret on leaving this life: that of having failed to carry out this fine resolve, when he considered its success guaranteed by the effort he had devoted to it.

Mme de Clèves, after leaving the lists, went to the Queen's, greatly preoccupied with what had happened. M. de Nemours arrived shortly afterwards, finely dressed, as though unaffected by his accident. If anything, he seemed uncommonly cheerful, and his joy at what he thought he had observed gave him an air that made him even more than usually attractive. Everybody was surprised at his entrance and no one failed to ask after his health, except Mme de Clèves who stayed by the fireplace and did not appear to see him. The King emerged from an inner room and, seeing him in the company, called him over to talk about his fall. M. de Nemours passed by Mme de Clèves and whispered:

'Today, madame, I was given a sign of your pity, but that is not what I most deserve.'

Mme de Clèves had guessed he had noticed her concern for

him and was proved right by these words. She had been very
disturbed at finding she was no longer able to hide her feelings
and at having revealed them to the Duc de Guise. She was
also much troubled by the fact that M. de Nemours knew of
them, but the regret was not unmixed with something akin to
pleasure.

The Reine Dauphine, most impatient to know what was in
the letter that Chastelart had given her, came over to Mme
de Clèves:

'Go and read this letter,' she said. 'It is addressed to M. de
Nemours and is evidently from that mistress for whom he
has abandoned all the rest. If you cannot read it at once,
keep it. Come to me this evening when I retire, to return it
and to tell me if you recognize the handwriting.'

At this, the Dauphine left Mme de Clèves, who was so
overcome that it was some time before she could move. Her
impatience and anxiety prevented her from staying longer at
the Queen's house: she left for home, though it was before
the time when she usually did so. She held the letter in a
trembling hand; her thoughts were so confused that she had
no clear thought at all; and she was in a state entirely new to
her, a kind of unbearable anguish unlike anything that she
had ever previously felt. As soon as she was in her room, she
opened the letter and found as follows:

I have loved you too much to allow you to think that the change
you see in me is due to inconstancy; I wish to tell you that it is
caused by your infidelity. You will be astonished to hear me speak
of your infidelity; you had concealed it so astutely from me, and I
have taken such care to hide my knowledge of it from you, that you
are rightly surprised to find that I know about it. I am myself
astonished at having been able to conceal the signs of this. No pain
has ever been so great as that I feel. I thought you were passionately
in love with me: I had ceased to hide my own passion for you and,
even at the moment when I allowed you every proof of it, I learned
that you were deceiving me, that you loved someone else and were
evidently sacrificing me to this new love. I realized it on the day of

the tilting at rings: this explains my absence. I pretended to be ill, to hide the turmoil in my mind; but I became ill in reality: my body could not bear such violent anguish. When I began to recover, I still pretended to be very sick, so that I might have an excuse for not seeing you or writing to you. I needed time to decide how I should act; twenty times, I made and unmade the same resolutions; but at last I decided you did not deserve to witness my suffering, and resolved to conceal it. I wanted to wound your pride, by letting you know that my feelings were diminishing of their own accord. In that way, I hoped to lessen the value of the sacrifice you made in rejecting them: I did not want you to have the pleasure of exhibiting how much I loved you, so that you might appear more attractive as a result. I resolved to write to you in a cool and listless manner, so that when you showed her the letters they would suggest the idea that it was possible to stop loving you. I did not want to give her the pleasure of finding out that I knew she had triumphed over me, or to increase her triumph by my despair and my rebukes. I thought that I should not punish you enough by breaking with you, and that I should inflict only a slight wound by ceasing to love you when you no longer loved me. It occurred to me that you would have to love me yourself to feel the pain that so cruelly tormented me: that of not being loved. I thought that, if there was one thing that might revive your feeling for me, it was to show you that my own feelings had changed; but to do so by pretending to hide the fact from you, as if I did not have the strength to admit it. I fixed on this resolve – but how difficult it was to make and, when I saw you again, how impossible it seemed to carry out! A hundred times, I was on the point of bursting into recriminations and tears: I was still in a state of health that served to disguise my distress and my anguish from you. From then on, I was sustained by the pleasure of using deception towards you as you had towards me; yet I was so unnaturally insistent in saying and writing that I loved you, that you noticed, sooner than I intended, how my feelings had changed. You were hurt, you reproached me for it. I tried to reassure you, but in so constrained a manner that you were still more convinced I no longer loved you. In short, I did everything I had meant to do. The capriciousness of your heart urged you towards me, the more you saw me distance myself from you. I enjoyed my vengeance to the full: it seemed you loved me more than ever and I showed that I no longer loved you. I had reason to believe you had altogether given up the person for whom you had left me, and also to be persuaded that you had never spoken about me to her; but your return and your discretion cannot make up for your infidelity. Your heart was divided between me and another; you deceived me. That is enough to deprive me of pleasure in being loved as I felt I deserved, and to confirm me in the resolution that so surprises you: never to see you again.

Mme de Clèves read and reread this letter several times, yet without knowing what it was she had read. All she could see was that M. de Nemours did not love her as she had believed, but that he loved other women and was deceiving them as he was her. What a thing that was to see and know for a person of her temperament, passionately in love, who had just displayed her feelings to a man whom she judged unworthy, and to another whom she had scorned for love of him! There could be no sharper or more bitter anguish than she felt, and it seemed to her that the acuteness of the pain derived from what had occurred during the day and that, if M. de Nemours had not had any reason to believe that she loved him, she would not have been troubled by his loving someone else. But she was wrong, for this pain that she found so unbearable was jealousy, with all the torments that it brings. From the letter, she saw that M. de Nemours had a long-standing affair. It seemed to her that the writer of the letter showed intelligence and character, and deserved to be loved; she admired her willpower, which she judged superior to her own, and envied the strength of mind that had enabled the woman to hide her feelings from M. de Nemours. From the end of the letter, she saw that the writer believed herself to be loved; and the idea occurred to her that the discretion the prince had shown, and which she had found so touching, was perhaps merely because of his love for this other, whom he did not want to displease. In fact, she had every thought that could increase her wretchedness and her despair. Bitterly she reproached herself, reflecting on her mother's advice! How much she regretted not having more stubbornly insisted upon leaving society, despite M. de Clèves, or for not having pursued her idea of telling him about her feelings for M. de Nemours! She thought it would have been better to disclose them to her husband – knowing his kindness and seeing it was in his interest to keep the secret – rather than reveal them to a man who was unworthy and unfaithful, who was perhaps using her, and only wanted her love to satisfy his pride and vanity. In short, she considered any misfortune and any extremity less than having shown M. de Nemours that she loved him, knowing that he loved someone else. Her one consolation was to think that, at least, knowing this, she had nothing more to fear from herself and that she would be entirely cured of her affection for the prince.

She disregarded the Dauphine's instruction to attend her on retiring. She took to her bed and pretended to be unwell, so that when M. de Clèves returned from court, he was told that she was asleep. She was, in reality, far from the ease of mind conducive to sleep. She passed the night doing nothing except to torment herself, rereading the letter she had been given.

Mme de Clèves was not the only person whose repose was disturbed by this letter. The Vidame de Chartres (for it was he, and not M. de Nemours, who had mislaid it) was in a state of extreme anxiety. He had spent the whole evening with M. de Guise, who had given a grand dinner for the Duc de Ferrare, his brother-in-law, and all the young people of the court. By chance, while they were at dinner, the conversation turned to well-composed letters. The Vidame de Chartres said that he had one on him that was finer than any that had ever been written. He was urged to show it, but declined. M. de Nemours pretended that he had no such thing and was merely boasting. The Vidame answered that this was testing his discretion to the limit; that nonetheless he would not show the letter, but read some passages of it from which they might judge that few men had ever received its like. At this, he tried to find the letter, but could not; he looked for it in vain, while they taunted him; but he was so visibly disturbed that they let the matter drop. He took his leave earlier than the rest, and hurried home impatiently to find out if he had left the missing letter behind. While he was still looking for it, one of the Queen's first footmen arrived, to tell him the Vicomtesse d'Uzès thought he should be advised immediately that people were saying at the Queen's house that he had dropped a love letter from his pocket at the tennis court; that they had described much of the content of the letter; that the Queen had been very curious to see it and had asked one of her courtiers to get it for her, but he replied that it had been entrusted to Chastelart.

The first footman told the Vidame de Chartres a number of other things that greatly concerned him. He left at once to visit a gentleman who was a close friend of Chastelart. He had him roused (though it was an extraordinary hour to ask for a letter), without saying who requested or who had lost it. Chastelart, convinced that it belonged to M. de Nemours and that he was in love with the Dauphine, had no doubt Nemours was the person asking for it to be returned. He took a malicious pleasure in sending the reply that he had entrusted the letter to the Dauphine: the man brought this answer to the Vidame de Chartres. This merely increased his concern and gave him new cause. After puzzling for a long time over what he should do, he decided that only M. de Nemours could help him out of his dilemma.

He went to his house and into his room. It was barely daybreak and the prince was sleeping calmly: what he had seen of Mme de Clèves the previous day had given him nothing but agreeable thoughts. He was very surprised at being woken up by the Vidame de Chartres, and asked if it was in revenge for what he had said over dinner that he had come to disturb his sleep. But the Vidame's face clearly showed that what had brought him was no jesting matter.

'I am here to confide in you the most important affair of

my life,' he said. 'I know quite well that you will not thank me for doing so, since I need your help; but I know too that I should forfeit your respect if I had told you what I am about to say, unless I were obliged to do so. I have lost the letter I mentioned yesterday evening: it is most vital that no one should know it was addressed to me. It was seen by several people who were at the tennis court where it fell out of my pocket. You were also there, and I beg you to let it be known that it was you who lost it.'

'You must think I have no mistress of my own,' M. de Nemours said, smiling, 'otherwise you would not make such a proposal or imagine that there is no one from whom I might be estranged, if she were to think that I receive such letters.'

'Please take me seriously, I beg you,' said the Vidame. 'If you have a mistress – and I am quite sure you do, though I have no idea who she is – you can easily exonerate yourself: I will give you everything you need to do so. And even if you did not exonerate yourself, the worst that could happen would be for you to fall out for a short time. But in my case, this business could dishonour someone who has loved me passionately and who is one of the most admirable women in the world; and, in addition, I risk becoming the object of an implacable hatred that will cost me my fortune and perhaps more besides.'

'I cannot follow everything that you are telling me,' M. de Nemours said, 'but you are implying that the rumour about a great princess, and her interest in you, was not altogether unfounded.'

'Nor was it,' answered the Vidame de Chartres, 'though I wish to God that it had been: I should not then be in my present predicament. But I shall have to tell you the full story, so that you may understand the danger I am in.

'Since I was first at court, the Queen[19] has always favoured me with her condescension and kindness, and I had reason to believe that she was well-disposed towards me. Yet there was nothing exceptional and it never occurred to me to have any feeling for her apart from respect. Indeed, I had a profound attachment to Mme de Thémines: seeing her, you can easily imagine that one could be much in love, if she felt the same, and so I was.

'Some two years ago, when the court was at Fontainebleau, I found myself two or three times talking to the Queen, on occasions when there were few others present. She seemed pleased by my conversation and responsive to everything I said. One day, in particular, we began to talk about trust. I said that there was no one who had my full confidence, that I thought a person would always repent of giving it, and that I knew many things I had never spoken about. The Queen told me that she respected me the more for it; that she had found no one in France able to keep a secret and was more inhibited by this than by anything, since it deprived her of the pleasure of imparting her confidence; and that it was necessary, in life, to have someone to whom one could talk, especially for those of her rank. On the following days, she returned several times to the topic, and even told me some private news. Finally, I concluded that she hoped to ensure my secrecy and wanted to confide in me. This idea drew me closer to her, I was touched by the mark of her favour and I paid court to her with much greater assiduity than before.

'One evening when the King and the ladies had gone riding in the forest, and she had declined because she felt slightly unwell, I stayed with her. She went down to the lakeside and dismissed her equerries in order to walk more freely, unsupported. After taking a short stroll, she came over to me and told me to follow her. "I wish to talk to you," she said. "And what I want to say will show you that I am a friend." At this, she paused; then, looking at me attentively, continued: "You are in love and, perhaps because you trust no one, you think that your love is a secret; but it is not; it is even known to some interested parties. You are observed: they know where you meet your mistress and plan to surprise you. I do not know who she is; I am not asking you; I only want to protect you against possible future misfortune." Observe, pray, the trap that the Queen had set for me and how hard it would have been not to fall into it. She wanted to know whether I was in love; but, by not asking who was the object of my feelings, and merely indicating that she meant to do me a favour, she gave me no cause to think that she had spoken out of personal interest or design.

'Despite that, and well-concealed as it was, I guessed the truth. I was in love with Mme de Thémines; but, even though she loved me, I was not fortunate enough to have any particular meeting-place where I saw her and might fear discovery; so I realized the Queen could not be speaking of her. I also knew that I had a liaison with another woman, who was less beautiful and less strait-laced than Mme de Thémines, and that it was possible someone might have discovered the place where we met; but, as I was not greatly concerned about her, it would be easy to protect myself against any sort of danger by no longer seeing her. So I preferred to admit nothing to the Queen, but to assure her, on the contrary, that I had long since given up any desire of being loved by those women whose love I might hope to win, since I considered them almost all undeserving of the affections of a self-respecting man, and that only someone far above them could engage my love. "You are not telling me the truth," the Queen answered. "I know that the opposite is the case. My manner of speaking obliges you to have no secrets from me. I should like to consider you one of my friends," she continued, "but, if I am to grant you that, I must not remain ignorant of your attachments. Consider if you wish to accede to that rank, at the cost of telling me about them. I am giving you two days to think about it; but, after that time, weigh your words and remember that, if I should subsequently find you have deceived me, I should never forgive you."

'At this, the Queen left me, without waiting for my reply. As you can imagine, my mind was greatly preoccupied with what she had said. The two days she had given me to think about it did not seem excessive to reach a decision. I could see that she wanted to know if I was in love and that she hoped I was not. I could see the consequences of the choice I was about to make. My vanity was not a little flattered by an intimate liaison with a queen, and one who is still extremely attractive. On the other hand, I loved Mme de Thémines and, though I was in a sense unfaithful to her with the other woman I mentioned, I could not make up my mind to break with her. I could also see the danger I ran in deceiving the Queen, and how difficult she was to deceive; yet I could not resolve to reject the opportunity that fate had offered me and decided to risk every consequence of my ill-conduct. I broke off the liaison which might be found out and hoped to conceal the one I had with Mme de Thémines.

'After the two days the Queen had given me, when I came into the room where all the ladies were assembled, she said aloud, in a voice that surprised me with its solemnity: "Have you thought of the matter I left with you, and do you know the truth of it?" "Yes, madame," I replied. "It is as I told Your Majesty." "Attend me this evening, when I am to do my writing," she went on, "and I shall give you my further instructions." I bowed deeply, without replying, and made certain to be there at the appointed time. I found her in the gallery with her secretary and one of her ladies.

'As soon as she saw me, she came up and led me to the far end. "Well," she said, "have you considered the matter well before telling me you have nothing to say, and does not my treatment of you merit a sincere reply?" "It is because I am speaking honestly to you, madame," I answered, "that I have nothing to tell you; and I swear to Your Majesty, with all the respect that I owe you, that I have no attachment for any lady of the court." "I should like to think so," the Queen answered, "because I hope so; and I hope so, because I wish you to be entirely devoted to me and because it would be impossible for me to feel happy with your friendship if you were in love. Those who are cannot be trusted; one cannot be sure of their confidentiality. They are too much distracted and divided, and their mistresses preoccupy their minds in a way that is incompatible with the kind of attachment I require of you. So remember it is on your word that you have no such liaison, that I have chosen to give you my trust. Remember that I want all of yours; that I do not wish you to have any friend, whether man or woman, of whom I do not approve; and that you are putting aside any consideration except that of pleasing me. I shall ensure that you do not suffer any disadvantage from this: I shall manage your affairs more conscientiously than you would yourself; and whatever I do for you, I shall feel only too well-rewarded if your conduct towards me proves to be as I hope. I have chosen you as the confidant of all my sorrows, and to help me to relieve them. As you may imagine, they are not inconsiderable. I may seem to endure the King's attachment to the Duchesse de Valentinois with little distress; but in reality I find it intolerable. She rules the King, she deceives him, she despises me, all my people are loyal to her. The Queen, my mother-in-law, proud of her beauty and of the pre-eminence of her uncles, pays me no respect. The Connétable de Montmorency is master of the King and of the kingdom; he hates me, and has given me proofs of his hatred that I cannot forget. The Maréchal de Saint-André is a bold young favourite, who treats me no better than the rest. If I were to describe my misfortunes in detail, you would weep; up to now I have not dared confide in anyone, but I am confiding in you; make sure that I never regret it and be my one consolation."

'As she said this, the Queen's eyes reddened; I was so truly moved by her favour that I almost fell at her feet. From that time, she trusted me absolutely; she did nothing without consulting me, and I enjoy an intimacy that has continued to this day.'

BOOK THREE

———◆———

'Much though my mind was absorbed by this new relationship with the Queen, an irresistible natural inclination drew me to Mme de Thémines. I felt that she was falling out of love with me. Good sense should have persuaded me to use this as the means to cure me of the liaison, but instead the change in her caused my love to increase and I acted so foolishly that the Queen came to hear word of the relationship. She belongs to a people naturally inclined to jealousy, and it could be that her feeling for me is more profound than she realizes. In any event, the rumour that I was in love was so unwelcome to her and caused her such distress that a hundred times I thought my case was lost. Eventually, by dint of much effort, submission and false promises, I reassured her; but I should not have been able to deceive her for long were it not that Mme de Thémines's own change of heart had released me in spite of myself. She showed that she no longer loved me, and I was so convinced of it that I was obliged not to pursue her further, but to leave her in peace. Some time later, she wrote me a letter, the same that I lost. From it, I learned that she knew about my liaison with the other woman I mentioned, which had caused the change in her.

'Since my feelings were no longer divided, the Queen was quite pleased with me; but since the feelings I have for her are not of a sort to preclude any other attachment, and since it is not by choice that one falls in love, I did so again, with Mme de Martigues, for whom I already felt a considerable liking when she was a Villemontais, a lady-in-waiting of the

Reine Dauphine. I have cause to believe that she does not find me unattractive, and she appreciates my discretion, though she does not precisely know the reason behind it. As far as she is concerned, the Queen suspects nothing: what she does suspect, however, is scarcely less troublesome. Since Mme de Martigues is always at the Dauphine's, I visit there much more frequently than before: the Queen has the notion that I am in love with the princess. The Dauphine's station is equal to her own, but she is superior in beauty and youth, so the Queen is beside herself with jealousy and can no longer disguise her hatred for her daughter-in-law. The Cardinal de Lorraine, who has in my view long aspired to the Queen's favour and sees me enjoying a place that he would wish to occupy, has intervened in the quarrel between them, on the pretext of healing the breach between her and the Dauphine. I am convinced he has discovered the real motive for the Queen's ill-feeling and I believe he is doing me every kind of disservice, without letting her see that he intends it.

'This is how things stand at present. Picture the effect of the letter I have lost, which ill-luck induced me to put in my pocket, intending to return it to Mme de Thémines. If the Queen sees that letter, she will know that I have deceived her and that, almost at the same time as I was deceiving her with Mme de Thémines, I was deceiving Mme de Thémines with another: imagine the idea that this will give her of me and whether she can ever trust me on my word. If she does not see that letter, what shall I tell her? She knows that it was handed to the Dauphine; she will think that Chastelart recognized the Dauphine's writing and that the letter is from her; she will conclude that the person whose jealousy is mentioned might be herself; in short, there is nothing that she will not have cause to suspect, and nothing that I shall not have cause to fear from her suspicions. Added to which, I have a fervent passion for Mme de Martigues. The Dauphine will certainly show her the letter and she will think that it was written recently, so I shall be equally at odds with the person whom I love most in the world, and the person in the world from whom I have most to fear. You can well see, in view of this, that I have good cause to beg you to say that the letter belongs to you, and to implore you to retrieve it from the Dauphine.'

'I can see,' said M. de Nemours, 'that one could hardly be in a greater predicament than yours, and you must admit you deserve it. I have been accused of infidelity in love and of involvement in several affairs at once; but you are so far ahead of me in this that I should not even contemplate embarking on anything to match what you have done. Did you think you could keep Mme de Thémines when you made a commitment to the Queen, and did you hope to commit yourself to the Queen, while managing to deceive her? She is a monarch, and an Italian one, who is consequently full of suspicion, jealousy and pride; yet when your good fortune (rather than your own good conduct) relieved you of your existing engagements, you entered into new ones and deluded yourself that, in the midst of the court, you could love Mme de Martigues without the Queen finding out. You should have made every effort to relieve her of shame at having taken the first step. She has an overwhelming passion for you, though you are too discreet to tell me so, or I to ask you; but she does love you, and is suspicious, and the facts are against you.'

'It is hardly your place to heap me with reproaches,' the Vidame interrupted. 'Your own experience should make you more indulgent towards my mistakes. Still, I admit that I am in the wrong; now just consider, please, how to extricate me from this pass. What I think you must do is to see the Reine Dauphine as soon as she is up, and ask her to return the letter, as being the person who lost it.'

'I have already told you,' M. de Nemours answered, 'that your suggestion is a trifle odd and that it might not be in my own best interests. But, apart from that, if the letter was seen to fall from your pocket, it might be hard to make anyone believe it came from mine.'

'I thought I told you,' the Vidame replied, 'that the Reine Dauphine was informed it had fallen out of yours.'

'What!' M. de Nemours exclaimed sharply, realizing in an instant the disservice such a misunderstanding might do him in the eyes of Mme de Clèves. 'Somebody told the Dauphine it was I who lost the letter?'

'They certainly did,' said the Vidame. 'And the cause of the error was that there were several of the Queens' courtiers in one of the rooms at the tennis court where our coats were left, when your servants and mine went to fetch them. That was when the letter fell out: the courtiers picked it up and read it aloud. Some thought it was yours, others mine. Chastelart, who took it and to whom I have just sent to ask for it, said that he had given it to the Dauphine, telling her it belonged to you, while those who spoke about it to the Queen unfortunately said it was mine; so you can easily do as I wish and help me out of this predicament.'

M. de Nemours had always been deeply attached to the Vidame de Chartres, and was still more fond of him because of his relationship to Mme de Clèves, but he could not take the risk of her hearing about the letter as something that concerned him. He began to think deeply and the Vidame, more or less guessing what was in his mind, said:

'I appreciate that you are afraid of falling out with the person you love, and I should even be inclined to think that this is the Reine Dauphine, except that you show so little jealousy of M. d'Anville, which suggests otherwise. In any event, it is right that you should not have to sacrifice your peace of mind for the sake of my own, so I am quite willing to give you the means of convincing this person that the letter was addressed to me, not to you: here is a note from Mme d'Amboise, a friend of Mme de Thémines, to whom she confided all her feelings for me. In it, Mme d'Amboise asks me to return her friend's letter, which is the one I have lost. My name is on the note, and its contents prove beyond doubt that the letter she requests is the same as the one that was found. I am entrusting this note to you and I give you leave to show it to your mistress to justify yourself. I beg you, do not lose any time, but go this morning to the Dauphine's.'

M. de Nemours promised the Vidame de Chartres that he would do so and took Mme d'Amboise's note; nonetheless, he did not plan to see the Dauphine, considering that he had a more pressing errand. He was certain that she would already have mentioned the letter to Mme de Clèves, and could not bear to think that a woman whom he loved so desperately should have reason to think he had any attachment to somebody else.

He went to her house at the time when he thought that she would be awake and sent to tell her that he would not request the honour of seeing her at such an extraordinary hour, unless impelled to do so by a matter of great importance. Mme de Clèves was still in bed, her spirit resentful and troubled by the sombre thoughts she had had during the night. She was very surprised when she learned that M. de Nemours was asking for her. She felt so ill-disposed towards him that she did not hesitate to say that she was unwell and could not speak to him.

The prince was unperturbed by her refusal: a certain coldness, at a time when she could be jealous, was not a bad sign. He went to M. de Clèves's room, and told him that he had just come from his wife's apartment and was very sorry not to have been able to see her, since he had to talk to her about an important matter on behalf of the Vidame de Chartres. He briefly indicated the gravity of the affair to M. de Clèves, who at once led him to his wife's room. If it had not been in darkness, she would have found it hard to conceal her alarm and astonishment at seeing M. de Nemours come in together with her husband. M. de Clèves told her that it was to do with a letter; that they needed her help on the Vidame's behalf; that M. de Nemours would tell her what had to be done; and that, for his part, he was going to see the King, who had just sent for him. M. de Nemours remained alone with Mme de Clèves, as he wished.

'Madame,' he said, 'I have come to ask if Mme la Dauphine happened to speak of a letter which Chastelart entrusted to her yesterday.'

'She did mention something to me,' Mme de Clèves replied, 'but I cannot think what this letter may have to do with my uncle and I can assure you his name does not appear in it.'

'That is true, madame,' answered M. de Nemours, 'he is not named in it; yet it is addressed to him and it is essential for him that you should retrieve it from the Dauphine.'

'I fail to understand,' Mme de Clèves said, 'why it should matter to him if this letter is seen, and why it has to be asked for under his name.'

'If you would be good enough to listen, madame,' replied M. de Nemours, 'I can soon enlighten you and tell you things which so deeply affect the Vidame's interests that I should not even have confided them to M. de Clèves, except that I needed his help in obtaining the honour of seeing you.'

'I think that everything you trouble to tell me will be in vain,' Mme de Clèves answered, somewhat tartly, 'and it would be better if you were to go to the Dauphine and, with no further ado, say what is your interest in the letter, since it happens she has already been told it is yours.'

The bitterness that M. de Nemours perceived in Mme de Clèves's heart gave him the most acute pleasure he had ever felt and outweighed his impatience to justify himself.

'I have no idea, madame,' he resumed, 'what anyone can have said to Mme la Dauphine, but I have no personal interest in this letter: it is addressed to the Vidame.'

'I believe you,' Mme de Clèves replied, 'but the Dauphine was told the contrary and she will hardly be persuaded that the Vidame's letters should fall out of your pocket. This is why, unless you have some reason which I do not know to conceal the truth from the Dauphine, I advise you to acknowledge it.'

'I have nothing to acknowledge,' he said. 'The letter is not addressed to me and, while there may be someone whom I should hope to convince of that fact, it is not the Dauphine. But, madame, since the fate of M. le Vidame is at stake here, please allow me to inform you of some things you should know.'

By her silence, Mme de Clèves showed she was willing to listen and M. de Nemours recounted, as briefly as he could, everything the Vidame had told him. Although these facts were of a kind to excite astonishment and deserve the listener's attention, Mme de Clèves heard him out with such extreme coolness that she seemed not really convinced of what he was saying, or else indifferent to it. This was her attitude until M. de Nemours mentioned the note from Mme d'Amboise, which was addressed to the Vidame de Chartres and supplied proof of everything he had said. Since Mme de Clèves knew that this person was a friend of Mme de Thémines, she found M. de Nemours's story had some plausibility, which made her think that the letter was perhaps not written to him. Suddenly, and in spite of herself, this idea dispelled the coldness that she had felt up to then. The prince, after reading out the note that proved what he was saying, gave it to her to read and told her that she would recognize the writing; she could not prevent herself from taking it, looking at the top to see it was addressed to the Vidame de Chartres and reading it from top to bottom to find out if the letter that Mme d'Amboise wanted was the same as the one in her possession. M. de Nemours went on to tell her everything he thought necessary to convince her; and, since one is easily convinced of a welcome truth, he persuaded Mme de Clèves that he had nothing to do with the letter.

At that, she turned to discussing the Vidame's dilemma and the danger he was in, reproving his misconduct and seeking how he could be helped. She expressed her astonishment at the Queen's behaviour and admitted to M. de Nemours that she had the letter: in short, as soon as she believed him innocent, she conversed calmly and openly on those same matters that she had previously scorned to listen to. They agreed that the letter must not be returned to the Reine Dauphine, in case she were to show it to Mme de Martigues, who knew Mme de Thémines's handwriting and who, because of her interest in the Vidame, would easily guess it was addressed to him. They also decided that the

Reine Dauphine should not be told everything concerning her mother-in-law, the Queen. With pleasure (since she had the excuse that it concerned her uncle's business) Mme de Clèves agreed to keep all the secrets M. de Nemours confided in her.

The prince would not have continued for ever speaking about the affairs of the Vidame de Chartres and this freedom to talk with her would have made him more audacious than he had yet dared to be, were it not that a message was brought to Mme de Clèves, commanding her to attend the Dauphine. M. de Nemours was obliged to leave; he went to the Vidame's to say that, after leaving him, he had thought it more appropriate to enquire of Mme de Clèves, being the Vidame's niece, rather than go directly to the Dauphine. There was good reason to approve his actions and to hope they would be crowned with success.

Meanwhile, Mme de Clèves dressed promptly to go to the Reine Dauphine's. No sooner had she entered the room than the Dauphine called her over and whispered:

'I have been expecting you for two hours and never have I been so hard put to disguise the truth as I was this morning. The Queen heard about the letter that I gave you yesterday, and she thinks it was the Vidame de Chartres who dropped it: you know she takes an interest in him. She had them look for the letter; she asked Chastelart for it, and he said that he had given it to me; so they came and asked me for it on the pretext that it was a fine letter which the Queen was curious to see. I did not dare say that you had it; I thought she would imagine I had entrusted it to you because of your uncle, the Vidame, and that he and I were closely in league with one another. I have already felt she was mortified at my seeing him so often. So I told her that the letter was in the clothes I was wearing yesterday and that the person who has my keys had gone out. Quickly give me the letter,' she continued, 'so that I can send it to her, and read it before sending, to see if I can recognize the hand.'

Mme de Clèves was more embarrassed than she had expected.

'I am not sure how you can, madame,' she replied, 'since M. de Clèves, to whom I gave it to read, gave it back to M. de Nemours, who came this morning to beg him to ask you for it. M. de Clèves was rash enough to mention that he had it and weak enough to give in to M. de Nemours's entreaties for its return.'

'You have put me in the most embarrassing situation possible,' the Dauphine answered, 'and you were wrong to give the letter back to M. de Nemours: since I gave it to you, you should not have returned it without my permission. What do you expect me to tell the Queen, and what will she think? She will have good grounds for believing that I am personally concerned in this letter and there is something between the Vidame and me. She will never be persuaded that the letter belongs to M. de Nemours.'

'I am most distressed,' Mme de Clèves said, 'at having put you in such a quandary. I can see how embarrassing it is, but it is M. de Clèves's fault and not mine.'

'On the contrary,' returned the Dauphine, 'it is your fault for giving him the letter: there is not a woman in the world except you who confides all that she knows in her husband.'

'I believe I was wrong, madame,' said Mme de Clèves. 'But think how to put right my mistake, instead of criticizing it.'

'Do you not remember, more or less, what was in the letter?' the Dauphine asked.

'Yes, madame,' she replied, 'I do: I read it more than once.'

'If that is so,' the Dauphine went on, 'you must go immediately and have it written out in an unrecognizable hand. I shall send it to the Queen: she will not show it to those who have already seen it. Or, even if she does, I shall continue to maintain it is the one I was given by Chastelart, and he will not dare to contradict me.'

Mme de Clèves agreed to this solution, particularly as she had the idea that she would send to M. de Nemours to have another sight of the letter itself, so that she could copy it word for word and have the writing imitated more or less

closely, thinking that this would certainly mislead the Queen.
As soon as she arrived home, she told her husband about the
Dauphine's dilemma and asked him to send for M. de
Nemours. This was done: he came post-haste. Mme de Clèves
recounted everything that she had already told her husband
and asked him for the letter, but M. de Nemours replied that
he had already returned it to the Vidame de Chartres, who
had been so overjoyed at having it and finding that he had
escaped the danger he was in, that he had instantly sent it
back to Mme de Thémines's friend. Mme de Clèves was now
in a fresh quandary. But, at last, after some discussion, they
decided to do the letter from memory. They shut themselves
up to work: orders were given at the door that no one should
be let in and all M. de Nemours's servants were sent away.
This atmosphere of intrigue and confidentiality had no slight
charm for the prince and even for Mme de Clèves. Her husband's presence and the involvement of the Vidame de
Chartres somehow overcame her misgivings. She knew only
the pleasure of seeing M. de Nemours, and felt a pure and
undiluted joy such as she had never before experienced: this
joy gave a freedom and animation to her spirits which M. de
Nemours had not previously seen in her, and which made
him love her still more. Never yet having enjoyed such pleasurable moments, he was full of vitality and wit: when Mme de
Clèves wished to start remembering the letter and writing it,
the prince, instead of helping her seriously, continually interrupted with amusing asides. Mme de Clèves responded in the
same spirit, so they had already been shut up together for a
long time, and twice messengers had come from the Dauphine
to tell Mme de Clèves to make haste, but they had not yet
half completed the letter.

M. de Nemours was quite content to prolong a time that
he found so agreeable, and forgot he was acting on behalf of
his friend. Mme de Clèves was not bored and similarly forgot
the interests of her uncle. In the end, the letter was hardly
completed by four o'clock, and so badly, the writing of the
copy looking so unlike that it was intended to imitate, that

the Queen must realize the truth unless she had very little
wish indeed to uncover it. So she was not deceived, despite
the care that was taken to convince her the letter was addressed to M. de Nemours. She not only remained convinced
that it belonged to the Vidame de Chartres, but she also
believed that the Dauphine was involved and that they had
some kind of understanding. This idea so greatly fuelled her
hatred for the Dauphine that she never forgave her, but
persecuted her until she had driven her out of France.

As for the Vidame de Chartres, he was ruined in her eyes
and – whether it was that the Cardinal of Lorraine had
already gained an ascendancy over her, or that the affair of
the letter, by showing her that she had been deceived, helped
to discover other deceptions that the Vidame had already
practised on her – one thing at least is certain: he could never
honestly make amends to her and their relationship came to
an end. Later, she ruined him over the Amboise conspiracy,[20]
in which he was involved.

When the letter had been sent to the Dauphine, M. de
Clèves and M. de Nemours went away, and Mme de Clèves
was left alone. As soon as she was no longer sustained by the
joy that one feels in the presence of what one loves, she
awoke as it were from a dream. She considered, with amazement, the huge difference between her state the evening
before, and her state then. She called to mind what bitterness
and coolness she had shown M. de Nemours when she still
believed Mme de Thémines's letter was addressed to him;
and what calm and sweetness had replaced that bitterness, as
soon as he persuaded her that the letter was nothing to do
with him. When she recalled that, the day before, she had
accused herself of a crime because she had given him signs of
her feelings – feelings that might have been inspired by com-
passion alone – and that, through her bitterness, she had
exhibited marks of jealousy that were most certainly proof of
love, she could no longer recognize herself. And when, moreover, she considered that M. de Nemours realized she knew
his feelings for her, and that he saw, too, in spite of her

knowing this, that she did not treat him ill, even in the presence of her husband, but on the contrary had never looked on him with such favour; and that it was because of her that M. de Clèves had sent to fetch him and that they had just spent an afternoon alone together, then she considered that she had an understanding with M. de Nemours and was deceiving the husband who least deserved it of any in the world; and she was ashamed to appear so little worthy of esteem, even in the eyes of her lover. But what she found harder to bear than all this, was the memory of the state in which she had spent the night and the agony she had suffered at the idea that M. de Nemours loved another, and that she was being deceived.

Until this time, she had experienced none of the mortal pangs of mistrust and jealousy. She had only thought to prevent herself from loving M. de Nemours and had not yet begun to fear that he might love someone else. Although her suspicions about the letter had been dispelled, they had still managed to open her eyes to the danger of being deceived and given her ideas of mistrust and jealousy that she had never before known. She was surprised at not having previously considered how unlikely it was that a man like M. de Nemours, who had always shown himself to be so frivolous in his dealings with women, might be capable of a sincere and lasting attachment. She thought it almost impossible that she should be satisfied with his love. 'And, even if I were to be,' she asked herself, 'what should I hope to do with it: tolerate it? Respond to it? Do I wish to become involved in an affair? To fail M. de Clèves? To fail myself? And do I wish, finally, to lay myself open to the bitter regrets and mortal agonies of love? I have been brought down and overcome by an impulse that is carrying me away in spite of myself. Every resolution on my part is useless: my thoughts were the same yesterday as they are today, yet I am doing today precisely the opposite of what yesterday I resolved. I must tear myself away from the presence of M. de Nemours, I must go to the country, however eccentric such a journey may seem; and, if M. de Clèves insists on preventing it or knowing the reason for it, perhaps I shall do him – and myself also – the disservice of telling him why.' She remained determined to follow this course and spent the evening at home, without going to find out from the Dauphine what had happened to the forgery of the Vidame's letter.

On M. de Clèves's return, she told him that she wanted to go to the country, that she was unwell and had a need to take the air. To M. de Clèves she seemed to possess a beauty that did not persuade him she was seriously ill. At first he made light of the proposed journey and replied that she was forgetting the forthcoming marriage of the princesses and the tournament: she had not long to prepare herself, if she was to appear with the same splendour as the other ladies. Her husband's arguments did not weaken her resolve. She begged him to agree that while he was away in Compiègne with the King, she should go to Coulommiers, a fine house one day's journey from Paris, which they were having expertly built for them. M. de Clèves consented and she left, with the intention of staying for some time, while the King set out for Compiègne where he was due to remain only a few days.

M. de Nemours had been greatly distressed at not seeing Mme de Clèves again since the afternoon which they had passed so agreeably and which had raised his hopes. His impatience to see her gave him no rest so that, when the King returned to Paris, he decided to visit his sister, the Duchesse de Mercoeur, who lived in the country, not far from Coulommiers. He invited the Vidame to accompany him. The latter readily accepted the invitation, which M. de Nemours made in the hope of seeing Mme de Clèves and calling on her with the Vidame.

Mme de Mercoeur welcomed them with much warmth and thought only how to amuse them and offer them all the pleasures of country life. While they were out stag-hunting, M. de Nemours wandered into the forest. Enquiring his way back, he learned that he was close to Coulommiers. Hearing the name, without further thought, or knowing what he intended to do, he rode off at full speed in the direction he had been shown. He arrived in the forest and allowed himself to be guided by chance along well-made roads, guessing they led to the château. At the end of the road he came across a pavilion, the lower floor of which consisted of a large drawing room flanked by two closets, the first opening on a flower garden, only separated by fencing from the woods, and the second looking down a broad avenue through the park. He went inside and would have stopped to admire the pavilion, were it not that he saw M. and Mme de Clèves coming along the avenue across the park, attended by a large number of servants. Since he had not expected to see M. de Clèves, whom he had left with the King, his first impulse was to hide. He went into the closet overlooking the flower garden, thinking to leave through a door that led into the forest. But, seeing that Mme de Clèves and her husband had sat down in the pavilion, while their servants remained in the park and would not approach him without going through the place where M. and Mme de Clèves had stopped, he could not resist the pleasure of seeing her or his curiosity to eavesdrop on her conversation with a husband who caused him more jealousy than any of his rivals.

He heard M. de Clèves say to his wife:

'But why do you not wish to return to Paris? What can keep you in the country? For some time now you have shown a fondness for solitude that surprises and pains me, since it keeps us apart. I even find you more than usually sad and I am afraid that you have some secret sorrow.'

'I have nothing distressing on my mind,' she answered, uneasily. 'But the turmoil of the court is so great and there are always so many people at your house, that it is inevitable one should grow weary in body and mind, and wish to rest.'

'Rest,' he replied, 'is hardly natural for someone of your age. Your activities, both at home and at court, are not such as to exhaust you, and what I find more worrying is that you may be only too pleased to be separated from me.'

'You would be most unjust, were you to think that,' she

returned, with increasing embarrassment. 'But I beg you to leave me here. If you could stay with me, I should be overjoyed, provided you stayed alone and did not want to be surrounded by that endless crowd of people, who hardly ever leave you.'

'Ah, madame!' M. de Clèves exclaimed. 'Your manner and your words tell me that you have some reason for wishing to be alone that I do not know, and I implore you to say what it is.'

He urged her for a long time to give him her reason, though he could not force her to do so. And, after resisting in a way that only excited his curiosity still further, she lapsed into a deep silence, with downcast eyes; then suddenly, looked up at him and spoke:

'Do not oblige me,' she said, 'to admit something to you that I do not have the strength to admit, though I have many times intended to do so. Only consider that it is unwise for a woman of my age, who is mistress of her own conduct, to remain exposed in the midst of the court.'

'What are you trying to suggest, madame?' M. de Clèves exclaimed. 'I am afraid that I might offend you if I were to put it in words.'

Mme de Clèves said nothing and her silence confirmed what her husband was thinking.

'You do not answer,' he went on. 'And that means that I am correct.'

'So be it, then,' she replied, throwing herself at his feet. 'I am going to make a confession to you that no wife has ever made to her husband; but the innocence of my conduct and of my intentions gives me strength. It is true that I have reason to leave the court and that I wish to avoid the dangers that sometimes threaten women of my age. I have never given the slightest sign of weakness and I should not fear to exhibit any if you were to allow me to retire from court, or if I still had Mme de Chartres's help to guide me. Perilous though it is, I am happy to take this course so that I may keep myself worthy to belong to you. I beg you a thousand times to forgive me, if my feelings displease you, but at least I shall never displease you by my actions. Consider that, to do what I am now doing, one must have more affection and esteem for a husband than a wife has ever had. Guide me, have pity on me, and love me still, if you can.'

Throughout this speech, M. de Clèves had remained with his head in his hands and beside himself, without thinking to help his wife up. When she stopped speaking, and he looked at her, seeing her at his feet, her face bathed in tears and of such incomparable beauty, he thought he would die of grief, and kissed her as he raised her to her feet:

'Have pity on me yourself, madame,' he said, 'since I deserve it; and forgive me if, in the first throes of so profound an anguish as I feel, I have not responded as I should to a conduct such as yours. You seem to me more worthy of esteem and admiration than any wife that lived; yet I think myself the most unfortunate of men. I have been passionately in love with you since the first moment I saw you; neither your severity, nor my possession of you could extinguish my love: it still endures. Yet I have never been able to inspire love in you, and I see that you are afraid you may feel it for someone else. Who is he, madame, this fortunate man who has caused you to fear? How long has he found favour with you? What has he done to attract you? What path has he discovered that led him to your heart? Not having reached it myself, I sought a kind of consolation in the idea that it was beyond reach. And now another has succeeded where I have failed. I suffer the jealousy both of a husband and of a lover; but it is impossible to feel a husband's jealousy after what you have done. Your conduct is too noble to give me any uncertainty; even as your lover, I am consoled by it. The confidence and sincerity that you show me are beyond price: you respect me enough to believe that I shall not abuse your trust. You are right, madame, I shall not abuse it, or love you any the less. You have made me unhappy by giving me the greatest proof of fidelity that ever wife gave her husband. But, please, have done and tell me who it is that you wish to avoid.'

'I beg you not to ask this of me,' she answered. 'I have determined not to tell you and I think that prudence requires me not to name him.'

'Have no fear,' said M. de Clèves. 'I know the world too well not to realize that consideration for a husband is no barrier to loving his wife. One must hate those who do so, but not reproach them; so, once more, madame, I implore you to tell me what I wish to know.'

'It will be pointless for you to insist,' Mme de Clèves went on. 'I have the strength to keep silent about something that I think I ought not to reveal. My confession was not the result of weakness, and admitting that truth requires more courage than attempting to conceal it.'

M. de Nemours heard every word of this conversation, and what Mme de Clèves had just said made him scarcely less jealous than her husband. He was so hopelessly in love with her that he thought everyone else must share this feeling. It was also true that he had several rivals, but he imagined himself to have still more, and he puzzled to think who this person might be that Mme de Clèves was speaking about. Several times he had thought himself not displeasing to her, but this impression was based on things that seemed so trivial to him at that moment, that he could not imagine he had awoken a passion so strong that it required her to resort to such extraordinary measures. He was so overwhelmed that he hardly knew what was before his eyes and he could not forgive M. de Clèves for not pressing his wife to give him the name that she refused to reveal.

Even so, M. de Clèves did all he could to learn it; and, after he had urged her in vain, she replied:

'I think you should be satisfied with my sincerity: do not ask more of me or give me cause to regret saying what I have. Be content with my repeated assurance that I have done nothing to reveal my feelings and that nothing has been done to me that might give me offence.'

'Oh, madame!' M. de Clèves suddenly exclaimed. 'I cannot believe you. I remember how confused you were, the day when your portrait was lost. You gave it away, madame – you gave away the portrait that was so dear to me and legitimately mine. You could not hide your feelings; you are in love, and he knows it; but so far your virtue has preserved you from anything beyond that.'

'Is it possible,' the princess replied, 'that you can believe there is any concealment in a confession such as mine, that nothing obliged me to make? Believe me; I have paid a high price for the trust that I ask of you. I beg you, believe that I did not give away my portrait; it is true that I saw it being taken, but I did not want to let it be known that I saw, in case I should lay myself open to hearing things that he has not yet dared to tell me.'

'So, how has he let it be known that he loves you?' M. de Clèves asked. 'And what signs of his love has he given you?'

'Spare me,' she replied, 'the pain of having to repeat to you details that make me ashamed to have noticed them and which have only too well convinced me of my own weakness.'

'You are right, madame,' he said, 'I am being unjust. Refuse me whenever I ask you such things, but do not be offended if I ask them.'

At this moment, several of their servants who had remained in the park, came to advise M. de Clèves that a gentleman had arrived for him from the King, requesting him to go to Paris that evening. M. de Clèves had to leave and could say nothing to his wife, except that he begged her to join him the next day and implored her to trust to the tenderness and respect that he felt for her, despite his affliction, and to be content with that.

When he had left and Mme de Clèves remained alone, and when she considered what she had just done, she was so appalled that she could hardly believe it was true. She thought that she had, of her own will, sacrificed the love and respect of her husband and that she had dug a pit for herself from which she would never escape. She wondered why she had done something so rash, and felt that she had embarked upon it almost without intending to do so. The peculiarity of her confession, for which she could see no precedent, made her realize how perilous it was.

But when she began to think that this remedy, drastic though it might be, was the only one that could protect her against M. de Nemours, she considered that she ought not to regret it and that the risk was not at all too great. She spent the whole night full of uncertainties, worries and fear, but at length her spirit regained its calm. She even felt some content-ment at having given this proof of her fidelity to a husband who was so deserving, who felt such respect and affection for her, and who had just provided her with still further evidence of this by the way in which he had reacted to her confession.

M. de Nemours, meanwhile, had left the place where he had overheard a conversation that affected him so pro-foundly, and made off into the forest. What Mme de Clèves said about her portrait restored him to life, by letting him know that he was the one whom she did not hate. At first, he gave way to this joy; but it lasted only a short time, when it occurred to him that, having just learned how he had touched her heart, he ought, by the same token, to be convinced that he would never be given any indication of it and that it was impossible to win over a woman who could follow so extra-ordinary a course. Yet he felt a decided pleasure at having reduced her to this extremity. He considered there was great merit in having gained the love of one so unlike all others of her sex; and, in short, he was infinitely happy and unhappy at the same time. Night overtook him in the forest and he had great difficulty in finding his way back to Mme de Mer-coeur's. He reached there as dawn broke and was at some-thing of a loss to explain what had delayed him. He did so as best he could and returned the same day to Paris with the Vidame.

He was so full of love and so surprised by what he had heard, that he committed a fairly common indiscretion, which is to speak in general terms of one's particular feelings and to describe one's own adventures under assumed names. On the return journey, he steered the conversation towards love and exalted the pleasures of being in love with a person who is deserving of one's affections. He mentioned the strange effects of that passion and finally, unable to suppress the astonishment he felt at Mme de Clèves's conduct, recounted it to the Vidame, without naming her or saying that he was involved; but he told the story with such enthusiasm that the Vidame easily guessed it concerned M. de Nemours. He strongly urged him to admit this. He said that he had known for a long time that the prince was deeply in love and that it was somewhat unfair to mistrust a man who had confided his life's secret to him. M. de Nemours was too much in love to confess it: he had always concealed it from the Vidame, even though he was fonder of him than of any man at court. He answered that one of his friends had told him the story and made him promise not to speak of it, begging him also to keep the secret. The Vidame assured him that he would not repeat it to anyone; yet M. de Nemours regretted having told him so much.

At the same time, M. de Clèves had gone to the King, smitten with mortal anguish. Never had any husband felt so passionately towards his wife or respected her so much. What he had discovered did not take away his esteem for her, but made it different in kind from what it had been until then. Most of all, he was obsessed with the wish to discover who had won her favour. M. de Nemours was the first person he thought of, as being the most attractive man at court; and also the Chevalier de Guise and the Maréchal de Saint-André, as two men who had thought they might win her and still paid her a good deal of attention: in this way he reached the conclusion that it must be one of these three. He arrived at the Louvre and the King led him into his study to say that he had been chosen to accompany Madame to Spain: he felt that no one would acquit himself better of the task and no one represent France so creditably as Mme de Clèves. M. de Clèves suitably accepted the honour of being chosen, and even thought of it as a means to remove his wife from the court without there appearing to be a change in her habits. Yet their departure was too distant for it to supply any remedy to his present trouble. He wrote immediately to Mme de Clèves, to tell her what the King had just said, also informing her of his urgent desire for her return to Paris. She did as he asked and when they saw each other, both were plunged into deep sorrow.

M. de Clèves addressed her as the most honourable man in the world and the one who best deserved what she had done:

'I am not in any way uneasy about your conduct,' he said. 'You have more strength and virtue than you think. So it is not fear of the future that distresses me. I am distressed only at seeing you have feelings for another that I have been unable to inspire in you.'

'I do not know what to say,' she answered. 'I am overwhelmed with shame when we talk about it. I beg you, spare me these cruel conversations; guide my conduct; ensure that I see nobody. That is all I ask. But allow me not to speak further of something that makes me feel so unworthy of you and which I find so unworthy of myself.'

'You are right, madame,' he replied. 'I am taking advantage of your good nature and your trust. But have some pity for the state into which you have plunged me and consider that, despite what you have told me, you are concealing a name that arouses unbearable curiosity in me. I do not ask you to satisfy it; yet I cannot resist telling you that I think the man whom I should envy is either the Maréchal de Saint-André, the Duc de Nemours or the Chevalier de Guise.'

'I shall not give you any answer,' she said, blushing, 'or any hint, in my answers, that might diminish or strengthen your suspicions. But if you attempt to confirm them by observing me, you will cause me an embarrassment that will be obvious to everybody. In heaven's name,' she went on, 'please allow me, on the excuse of some illness or other, to see no one.'

'No, madame,' he replied. 'It would soon be discovered that that was merely a pretext; and, in any case, I wish to trust nothing except yourself: this is the course that my heart advises me to take, and reason concurs. In your present mood, by allowing you your freedom, I am setting you narrower bounds than I could lay down for you myself.'

M. de Clèves was not mistaken: the trust that he showed his wife strengthened her still further against M. de Nemours and drove her to even greater resolve than any constraint could have done. So she went to the Louvre and to the Dauphine's as usual, but so studiously avoided the presence and the eyes of M. de Nemours that she almost deprived him of all the joy he had in believing himself to be loved by her. He saw nothing in her actions that did not persuade him to the contrary. He almost doubted that what he had heard might not be a dream, so unlikely did it appear. The only thing that reassured him he had not made a mistake was the immense sadness of Mme de Clèves, much as she tried to disguise it: it may be that pleasant looks and sweet words would not have increased M. de Nemours's love to such an extent as this self-denying behaviour.

One evening when M. and Mme de Clèves were at the Queen's, someone mentioned a rumour that the King was to appoint another nobleman of the court to accompany Madame to Spain. M. de Clèves was watching his wife as they added that it could be either the Chevalier de Guise or the Maréchal de Saint-André. He noticed that she gave no sign of emotion on hearing these names, or the proposal that they might make the journey with her. This led him to think that neither one was the man whose presence she feared and, wishing to confirm his suspicions, he went into the Queen's study, where the King was. After staying there for some time, he returned to his wife and whispered to her that he had just learned it was M. de Nemours who would go with them to Spain.

M. de Nemours's name and the idea of being obliged to see him daily throughout a long journey, in her husband's presence, so greatly disturbed Mme de Clèves that she could not hide her emotion; so, wishing to supply an excuse for it:

'It is very unpleasant for you,' she said, 'that this prince has been chosen. He will share all the honours and I think you should try to have someone else put in his place.'

'It is nothing connected with my reputation, madame,' he answered, 'that makes you afraid that M. de Nemours might accompany me. You are vexed at the news for another reason. This vexation tells me what I should have learned from any other woman through the pleasure that she would have expressed. But fear nothing: what I have just told you is untrue; I made it up, to confirm something that I already suspected only too well.'

Whereupon he left, seeing his wife's extreme confusion, and not wishing to add to it by remaining.

At that moment, M. de Nemours came in and at once noticed Mme de Clèves's state. He went over to her and whispered that, out of respect, he did not dare ask what made her more distracted than usual. M. de Nemours's voice brought her back to herself and, looking at him, not having heard what he had just said, full of her own thoughts and of the fear that her husband might see them together:

'In heaven's name,' she exclaimed, 'leave me in peace!'

'Alas, madame,' he replied, 'I do, and only too much. What complaint can you have? I dare not speak to you, I dare not even look at you, I approach you only with trepidation. What have I done to deserve what you have just said, and why do you suggest that I am somehow responsible for the unhappiness I see in you?'

Mme de Clèves was very annoyed at having given M. de Nemours an opportunity to express himself more openly than ever in his life. She left him without answering and returned home, her mind more troubled than it had ever been. Her husband plainly saw that she was in a greater state of confusion. He observed that she was afraid he would speak of what had occurred. She went into a parlour and he followed her.

'Do not try to avoid me, madame,' he said. 'I shall say nothing that might distress you; and I beg your forgiveness for the shock that I gave you just now. I have been sufficiently punished for it by what I learned. Of all men, M. de Nemours was the one I feared most. I can see the perils of your situation: be strong, for love of yourself and, if possible, for love of me. I do not ask this of you as a husband, but as a man whose happiness depends on you, and who loves you more tenderly and more passionately than the one your heart prefers.'

M. de Clèves was overcome with emotion and could hardly finish what he was saying. His wife appreciated how he felt and, bursting into tears, kissed him with such tenderness and sorrow that he was left in a state little different from hers. For some time they remained in silence and parted without having the strength to speak to each other.

The preparations for Madame's marriage were concluded. The Duc d'Albe[21] arrived for the ceremony. He was greeted with every form of pomp and magnificence imaginable on such an occasion. The King sent out the Prince de Condé, the Cardinals de Lorraine and Guise, the Ducs de Lorraine, Ferrare, Aumale, Bouillon, Guise and Nemours to welcome him. They were attended by many gentlemen and a great number of pages in livery. The King himself received the Duc d'Albe at the main gate of the Louvre, with the two hundred gentlemen-in-waiting and the Connétable at their head. When the duke approached the King, he tried to embrace his knees, but the King restrained him, and made him walk by his side up to the Queen and Madame, for whom the Duc d'Albe had brought a magnificent present on his master's behalf. He afterwards went to Mme Marguerite, the King's sister, to offer M. de Savoie's compliments and to assure her that he would be arriving in a few days' time. Huge receptions were held at the Louvre to show off the ladies of the court to the Duc d'Albe and the Prince d'Orange who was accompanying him.

Much though she would have liked to, Mme de Clèves dared not absent herself for fear of displeasing her husband, who positively ordered her to attend. She was still further persuaded by the absence of M. de Nemours. He had gone to receive M. de Savoie and, when the prince arrived, was obliged to remain almost always by his side to help him with everything concerning the marriage ceremony. Consequently, Mme de Clèves did not meet him as often as usual, which brought her a kind of tranquillity.

The Vidame de Chartres had not forgotten his conversation with M. de Nemours. He still held to the idea that the adventure the prince had described was his own and he observed him so closely that he might perhaps have uncovered the truth, had it not been that the arrival of the Duc d'Albe and M. de Savoie caused such changes and activity in the court that it prevented him seeing anything that might have enlightened him. The desire for enlightenment, or rather a natural tendency to tell all that one knows to the person one loves, induced him to mention to Mme de Martigues the extraordinary case of this woman who had confessed to her husband the passion that she felt for another. He assured her that M. de Nemours was the one who had inspired this overwhelming love and he begged her to help him by observing the prince. Mme de Martigues was delighted to learn what the Vidame told her, and the curiosity that she had always observed in the Dauphine about everything concerning M. de Nemours made her still more eager to discover the truth.

A few days before the one chosen for the marriage ceremony, the Dauphine held a dinner for her father-in-law, the King, and for the Duchesse de Valentinois. Mme de Clèves, who had been busy dressing, went to the Louvre later than usual. On her way she met a gentleman who had come to look for her at the Dauphine's request, and when she entered the room, the Dauphine called to her, from the bed on which she was lying, to say that she had been very impatient to see her.

'I suppose, madame,' Mme de Clèves replied, 'that I should not thank you for this impatience, and that it is caused by something other than the simple desire to see me.'

'Indeed, it is,' answered the Dauphine, 'but despite that you should be obliged to me, since I am about to tell you a story that I am certain you will be pleased to learn.'

Mme de Clèves knelt by the bed and, luckily for her, her face was in shadow.

'You remember,' the Dauphine said, 'how eager we were to discover what had caused the change in M. de Nemours: I think I know the answer, and it will surprise you. He is desperately in love and himself deeply loved by one of the most beautiful women at court.'

These words, which Mme de Clèves could not think would apply to herself, since she believed no one knew of her love for M. de Nemours, caused her an anguish that can well be imagined.

'I can see nothing surprising in that,' she replied, 'in a man of M. de Nemours's age and one so handsome as he is.'

'That is not what you ought to find surprising,' the Dauphine went on, 'but when you learn that this woman who loves M. de Nemours has never given him any indication of it, and her fear that she might not be able to remain in control of her passion has induced her to confess it to her husband, so that he might remove her from the court. And it is M. de Nemours himself who passed on what I have just said.'

At first Mme de Clèves had suffered at the idea she was not implicated in the story, but the Dauphine's last words caused her to suffer despair at the certainty that she was only too directly involved. She was unable to reply and remained with her head against the bed while the Dauphine continued to speak, so caught up in what she was saying that she did not notice Mme de Clèves's confusion. When she was more in control of herself, she said:

'Madame, this story seems somewhat improbable to me, and I would like to know who told it to you.'

'It was Mme de Martigues,' the Dauphine replied, 'and she had it from the Vidame de Chartres. You know that he is in love with her; he told it to her as a secret that he learned from the Duc de Nemours himself. It is true that M. de Nemours did not tell him the lady's name and did not even admit that he himself was the object of her love; but the Vidame de Chartres has no doubt about it.'

As the Dauphine was saying this, somebody came over to the bed. Mme de Clèves's head was turned in such a way that she could not see who it was; but she knew perfectly well when the Dauphine exclaimed, in a tone of merriment and surprise:

'Here is the man himself, and I mean to ask him about it.'

Mme de Clèves correctly guessed that it was the Duc de Nemours, even without turning towards him. She quickly moved closer to the Dauphine and whispered that she should be careful not to say anything about the matter; he had confided it to the Vidame de Chartres, and it might lead to a quarrel between them. The Dauphine laughed and answered that she was too discreet for that, then turned back to M. de Nemours. He was dressed for the evening's reception and, speaking with his innate charm of manner, said:

'I believe, madame, that I may, without temerity, presume you were speaking of me when I entered, that you intended to ask me something and that Mme de Clèves is opposed to your doing so.'

'You are right,' the Dauphine replied. 'But I shall not comply with her wishes as I usually do. I want you to tell me if a story that I have heard is true and if you are not the person who is in love with, and loved by a woman of the court who has been careful to conceal her feelings from you, but has confessed them to her husband.'

It is impossible to imagine Mme de Clèves's confusion and embarrassment: if death had come to relieve her from that state, she would have welcomed it. But M. de Nemours was, if anything, more embarrassed. What he had just heard from the Dauphine who, he had reason to believe, was not indifferent to him, in the presence of Mme de Clèves, the person at court in whom she had the greatest trust and who also returned it, caused such a tumult of confused ideas in his mind that he was quite unable to control his expression. The distress he witnessed in Mme de Clèves, through his fault, and the thought that he had given her good cause to hate him, overwhelmed him to such an extent that he was speechless. The Dauphine, seeing him unable to reply, said to Mme de Clèves:

'Look at him! Look at him, and tell me if he is not the person concerned.'

However, M. de Nemours, overcoming his first confusion and seeing how important it was to extricate himself from such a pass, suddenly regained control of his thoughts and his expression:

'I admit, madame,' he said, 'that no one could be more surprised, or upset than I am by the Vidame de Chartres's betrayal, in passing on the secret of what happened to one of my friends after I had confided it to him. I could have my revenge on him,' he continued, smiling calmly in a way that almost dispelled the Dauphine's suspicions. 'He has told me things, in confidence, which are of no small significance. But I cannot think, madame,' he continued, 'why you do me the honour of implicating me in this matter. The Vidame cannot say that it concerns me, since I told him the opposite. I might claim to be a man in love; but as for being a man loved, I do not think, madame, that this is a thing you can attribute to me.'

The prince was pleased at being able to say something to the Dauphine that had a connection with what he had previously intimated to her, to turn her mind away from any ideas that she might have. She also thought that she understood what he meant, but continued to play on his embarrassment.

'I was concerned, madame,' he told her, 'for my friend's interests and because he might justifiably reproach me with having repeated a secret that is dearer to him than life itself. Even so, he confided no more than a part of the story to me, and did not name the person whom he loves. I only know that he is the man most in love and most to be pitied in the world.'

'Do you consider he should be pitied,' the Dauphine retorted, 'because he is loved?'

'Do you think that he is, madame,' he answered, 'and that someone who truly loved him would tell her husband about it? Doubtless she knows nothing of love and what she feels for him is mere gratitude for the passion he feels for her. My friend cannot flatter himself that he has anything to hope; but, unhappy though he is, he is happy at least in having inspired this fear of loving him and he would not change his place for that of the most fortunate lover in the world.'

'Your friend's passion is easily satisfied,' the Dauphine said, 'and I am starting to think that you are not referring to yourself. In fact,' she went on, 'I am almost inclined to agree with Mme de Clèves when she claims that this story cannot be true.'

'Indeed, I think it cannot be,' said Mme de Clèves, who had not yet spoken. 'And, even if it were so, how could anyone have learned about it? It is hardly likely that a woman who was capable of such an extraordinary action, should be weak enough to talk about it; and it is improbable that her husband would mention it, either, or he would be a husband very undeserving of the trust she had shown him.'

M. de Nemours, realizing that Mme de Clèves suspected her husband, was quite happy to confirm her suspicions. He knew that M. de Clèves was the most formidable rival in his path.

'Jealousy,' he said, 'and a curiosity, perhaps, to discover more about the matter than he has been told, can lead a husband to do some very rash things.'

Mme de Clèves had reached the end of her strength and her resolve; and, unable to bear this conversation any longer, she was about to say that she felt ill when, happily for her, the Duchesse de Valentinois entered and told the Dauphine that the King was on his way. The Dauphine retired to her chamber to dress and, as Mme de Clèves was on the point of following her, M. de Nemours came over.

'I should give my life, madame,' he said, 'to speak to you

for a moment. But, among all the important things I have to tell you, I consider none more so than to beg you to believe that if I said anything that the Dauphine might apply to herself, I did so for reasons that do not concern her.'

Mme de Clèves pretended not to hear this; she left without looking at him and began to follow the King who had then entered. As there was a large throng of people, she tripped on the train of her dress and stumbled: she used this as an excuse to escape from a place where she did not feel she had the strength to stay, and returned home.

M. de Clèves arrived at the Louvre and was surprised not to find his wife there: they informed him of her accident. He went home at once to learn how she was, found her in bed and realized that she was not badly hurt. When he had spent some time at her side, he was surprised to observe she was feeling profoundly unhappy.

'What is wrong, madame?' he said. 'I think you must be suffering some other pain, apart from the one you complain of?'

'I am as deeply wounded as I could possibly be,' she replied. 'What have you done with the extraordinary – or, rather, the insane – trust that I showed by confiding in you? Did I not deserve your secrecy, or even if not, was it not in your own interest? Did your curiosity to know a name that I cannot reveal to you, impel you to confide in someone, in an attempt to discover it? This curiosity alone can have driven you to such a cruelly rash act, the consequences of which are as disastrous as can be. The matter is out: it has just been told to me, without knowing that I was the person mainly concerned.'

'What are you saying, madame?' he exclaimed. 'Do you accuse me of having told someone about what passed between us, and are you telling me it is public knowledge? I am not going to defend myself against the charge of having repeated it; you would not believe me, though no doubt you must have applied something to yourself that was being told you about somebody else.'

'Oh, sir,' she replied, 'there is no other story in the world similar to mine; there is no other woman capable of what I have done. It cannot have been invented by chance: it was never imagined and the idea never entered another head than my own. The Dauphine has just told me the whole story: she learned it from the Vidame de Chartres, who had it from M. de Nemours.'

'M. de Nemours!' cried M. de Clèves, with a gesture of passion and despair. 'What! Does M. de Nemours know that you love him, and that I know it?'

'You always choose M. de Nemours, rather than anyone else,' she answered. 'I have told you that I shall never give you an answer to your suspicions. I am not sure whether M. de Nemours knows my part in this story, or the one that you have attributed to him; but he told it to the Vidame de Chartres, saying that he had it from one of his friends, who had not named the woman. This friend of M. de Nemours must belong to your circle: you confided in him, in an attempt to satisfy your curiosity.'

'Is there a friend in the world to whom one would wish to confide such a secret?' M. de Clèves replied. 'And would anyone want to satisfy his curiosity at the cost of telling someone else a thing that he would wish to conceal even from himself? It is rather for you, madame, to consider to whom you have been speaking: it is more likely that the secret was revealed by you than by me. Unable to endure your plight alone, you sought the commiseration of some confidante who has betrayed you.'

'Do not crush me entirely!' she cried. 'Do not be cruel enough to accuse me of an offence you have yourself committed. Can you possibly suspect me, and having brought myself to speak to you, would I be able to speak to somebody else?'

Mme de Clèves had given such convincing proof of her honesty by confessing to her husband, and she so vehemently denied confiding in anyone, that he did not know what to think. On the other hand, he was certain that he had said nothing himself; this was not a thing that could be guessed at, it must be known; so the knowledge came necessarily from one of them; but what caused him the sharpest anguish was knowing that the secret was in the possession of a third party and would soon, surely, be public.

Mme de Clèves was thinking along much the same lines: she considered it equally impossible that her husband should have talked, and that he should not have done so. What M. de Nemours had said, about curiosity leading a husband to do something rash, seemed so readily applicable to M. de Clèves's case that she had to believe it was not a remark inspired by mere chance; and this likelihood persuaded her that M. de Clèves had abused her trust in him. They were both so preoccupied with their own thoughts that they remained a long time without speaking, and only broke this silence to repeat things that they had already said many times; and they were left more distant and more estranged in heart and mind than they had ever been.

It is easy to imagine the state in which they spent the night. M. de Clèves had exhausted all fortitude in supporting the misery of seeing a wife whom he adored swayed by her passion for another man. He had no further strength, and thought he should not even find it in circumstances which were so damaging to his honour and his good name. He did not know what to think of his wife; he could not decide what conduct he should prescribe for her, or how he should conduct himself; on all sides, he could see only gulfs and precipices. At length, after a long period of fretting and perplexity, realizing that he had shortly to go to Spain, he resolved to do nothing that might fuel suspicion or knowledge of his wretched state. He went to Mme de Clèves and told her that the question was not to discover which of them had given away the secret, but to show that what was being said was an invention, and that she was not involved; that it was up to her to persuade M. de Nemours and the others of this; that she had only to behave towards him with the distance and coldness that she ought to show a man who expressed love for her; that, in this way, she could easily dispel any idea he might have that she was attracted to him; that she should not therefore be distressed by whatever he might previously have thought because if, from then on, she gave no sign of weakness, all such thoughts would rapidly disappear; and that, above all, she must go to the Louvre and to every assembly, as she was in the habit of doing.

At this, M. de Clèves left his wife without waiting for her reply. She thought that there was a lot of truth in what he said, and her anger towards M. de Nemours made her believe that she would find it very easy to do as he suggested; but she anticipated that it would be hard to attend all the marriage ceremonies and appear with a calm face and an untroubled mind. However, since she was to wear the Dauphine's dress, and this was an honour for which she had been preferred over several other ladies at court, it was impossible to refuse without causing a great deal of gossip and looking for explanations. So she resolved to be firm with herself, though she took the remainder of that day to prepare and abandon herself to all the feelings that were troubling her mind. She shut herself up alone in her chamber. Of all her ills, the one that most overwhelmed her, was having cause to blame M. de Nemours, and finding no reason to excuse him. She could not doubt that he had told the story to the Vidame de Chartres: he had admitted as much; nor could she doubt also, from the manner in which he had spoken of it, that he knew the matter concerned her. How could she forgive such imprudence, and what had become of the prince's unusual discretion, which she had found so appealing?

'He was discreet,' she thought, 'so long as he believed in his misfortune; but one glimpse of happiness, however uncertain, put an end to discretion. He could not imagine himself to be loved, without wishing to let it be known. He said everything that it was possible for him to say: I did not confess that he was the man I loved, but he suspected it and revealed his suspicions. Had he been certain of it, he would have behaved in the same way. I was wrong to imagine that any man could be found who was able to conceal something that flattered his reputation. Yet it is for the sake of this man, whom I believed so different to other men, that I have become like others of my sex, when I am so far from resembling them. I have lost the love and respect of a husband who ought to have ensured my happiness. I shall soon be generally regarded as someone possessed by a foolish and uncontrollable passion. The man for whom I feel this is no longer unaware of it; yet it was to avoid this misfortune that I risked my peace of mind, and even my life.'

These sad thoughts were drowned in a gush of tears; but whatever sorrow might overwhelm her, she knew she would have had the strength to bear it, if she had been contented with M. de Nemours's conduct.

The prince's own state of mind was no better. His indiscretion in speaking to the Vidame de Chartres, and the lamentable consequences of that indiscretion, caused him mortal anguish. He could not recall the distress, anxiety and affliction in which he had seen Mme de Clèves, without being overcome by it. He was inconsolable at having said certain things to her about the matter which, pleasant and charming though they may have been in themselves, seemed to him at that moment coarse and ill-mannered, since they had given Mme de Clèves to understand that he knew she was this woman who was passionately in love, and he the object of her passion. All that he could desire was an opportunity to talk to her; but he felt this was something he ought rather to fear than to wish.

'What should I have to tell her?' he wondered. 'Should I make further demonstration of what I have indicated to her only too clearly? Should I let her see that I know she loves me, when I have never even dared to tell her that I love her myself? Should I start to speak openly of my feelings, so that I will seem like a man emboldened by hope? Can I even consider going near her and daring to give her the anguish of having to bear the sight of me? How could I justify myself? I have no excuse, I am unworthy that Mme de Clèves should look at me, and hence do not hope that she will ever look at me again. Through my error, I have only given her still better means to protect herself against me than any she was seeking and, perhaps, seeking in vain. My foolishness has lost me the happiness and the distinction of being loved by the most lovable person in the world and the most worthy of love; but, had I lost this happiness without her having to suffer and without having inflicted this mortal pain on her, that would be a consolation to me; for, at this moment, I am suffering more from the harm I have done her, than from that I have done myself in her eyes.'

M. de Nemours spent a long time with such distressing thoughts. He felt a recurrent desire to speak to Mme de Clèves. He considered how to find the means and thought of writing to her; but at last felt that, after the error he had committed and the mood she must be in, the best he could do would be to indicate his deep respect by his sorrow and his silence, even showing her that he did not dare come before her, and to wait for whatever time, chance and her liking for him might do in his favour. He also decided not to reprimand the Vidame de Chartres for his betrayal, in case this should reinforce his suspicions.

The court was so preoccupied by Madame's betrothal, which was to take place the following day, and by the wedding, the day after, that Mme de Clèves and M. de Nemours found it easy to hide their sadness and their anguish from public scrutiny. Even the Dauphine only spoke in passing to Mme de Clèves of their conversation with M. de Nemours, and M. de Clèves deliberately made no mention of anything that had occurred, so that she was less embarrassed by it than she had expected.

The betrothal was held at the Louvre and, after the feast and the ball, the whole of the royal household went to spend the night, according to custom, at the bishop's palace. In the morning, the Duc d'Albe, who only ever dressed very simply, put on a coat of gold cloth shot with the colour of fire and with yellow and black, encrusted with precious stones; he wore a closed crown on his head. The Prince d'Orange, no less magnificently dressed and attended in livery, and all the Spaniards followed by their servants, came to escort the Duc d'Albe from the Hôtel de Villeroi where he was staying, and set out, walking four by four, until they reached the bishop's palace. As soon as he had arrived, they proceeded by rank to the church: the King leading Madame who also had a closed crown and her train supported by Mlle de Montpensier and Mlle de Longueville. The Queen walked behind, without a crown. After her, came the Reine Dauphine, Madame, the King's sister, Mme de Lorraine and the Queen of Navarre, their trains supported by princesses. The Queens and the princesses all had their ladies-in-waiting splendidly attired in the same colours as themselves, so that you could know whose ladies they were by the colours in which they were dressed. They went up on to the dais that had been erected in the church and the marriage ceremony took place. Then they returned to dine at the bishop's palace and, at five o'clock, left for the palace itself where the feast was to be held to which Parliament, the royal courts and the nobility of the town had been invited. The King, the Queens, princes and princesses ate at the marble table in the great hall of the palace, with the Duc d'Albe seated beside the new Queen of Spain. Beneath the steps leading to the marble table and on the King's right hand was a table for the ambassadors, arch-bishops and knights of the order; on the other side, a table for members of the Parliament.

The Duc de Guise, wearing a costume fringed with gold, served the King as Grand Master; the Prince de Condé as Steward; and the Duc de Nemours as Cupbearer. After the tables were removed, the ball began. There was an interlude for ballets and *tableaux vivants*, with theatrical machines, then the dancing resumed. At length, after midnight, the King and all the court returned to the Louvre. Sad though she was, Mme de Clèves appeared to everyone, and especially to M. de Nemours, incomparably beautiful. He dared not speak to her, though the crush at the ceremony gave him several opportunities; but he showed her such sadness in his looks and held back with such respectful timidity from approaching her, that she no longer believed him guilty, though he had said nothing to justify himself. On subsequent days, his conduct was the same and this same conduct had the same effect on the heart of Mme de Clèves.

At last, the day came for the joust. The Queens took their places in the galleries and on the rostra prepared for them. The four champions appeared at the ends of the lists, with an assemblage of horses and liveries that composed the finest spectacle ever to be seen in France.

The King had no colours other than white and black, which he always wore in deference to the widowhood of Mme de Valentinois. M. de Ferrare and all his attendants were in yellow and red; M. de Guise appeared in crimson and white: at first, the reason for his wearing these colours was not known; but it was recalled that they were those of a beauty whom he had loved when she was still unmarried and loved still, though he no longer dared declare it to her. M. de Nemours was in yellow and black; they tried to learn why, but in vain. Mme de Clèves had no difficulty in guessing: she remembered having said in his presence that she liked yellow and was sorry to be a blonde, since she could not wear that colour. He considered he could appear in it without indiscretion since, as Mme de Clèves did not use it, no one would suspect it of being hers.

Never had so much skill been shown as by the four champions. Though the King was the best horseman in the realm, it was not clear to anyone on this occasion who had the advantage. M. de Nemours exhibited a grace in his every action that might have tipped the balance in his favour even among those less directly interested than Mme de Clèves. As soon as she saw him appear at the end of the lists, she was overwhelmed with emotion; and, whenever the prince was engaged in combat, she had difficulty in concealing her joy, if he carried it off with success.

In the evening, when everything was almost done and they were ready to retire, the King (to the great misfortune of his country) declared he would break one more lance. He called on the Comte de Montgomery, who was a very skilful jouster, to take his place in the lists. The count begged the King to excuse him and put forward every argument he could find, but the King, on the verge of anger, sent to tell him that he was adamant. The Queen let the King know that she implored him to desist: he had done so well that he should be content and she begged him to return to her side. He answered that it was for love of her that he wished to joust on, and entered the field. She sent back M. de Savoie, to ask him once more to return; but in vain. He charged, the lances broke and a splinter from the Comte de Montgomery's flew off into the King's eye and lodged there. He fell instantly, and his squires and M. de Montmorency, who was one of the marshals of the field, ran to him. They were amazed at the extent of the wound, but the King showed no surprise. He said it was only slight, and that he forgave the count. One can imagine what anxiety and sorrow this unhappy accident caused, on a day that had been marked out for happiness. As soon as the King had been taken to his bed, the surgeons examined his wound and declared it to be very dangerous. The Connétable at that moment remembered the prediction made to the King, that he would be killed in single combat, and did not doubt it had come to pass as foretold.

The accident was reported to the King of Spain, at that time in Brussels, who sent his own doctor, a man of great repute; but he pronounced the King's case hopeless.

There was no slight commotion in a court which was thus divided and rent by so many opposing factions, at the prospect of such an important event. Yet all these currents were hidden and there was no sign of concern apart from the one anxiety with the health of the King. The Queens, princes and princesses hardly left the antechamber of his room.

Knowing that she was obliged to be there, that she would see M. de Nemours, that her embarrassment at seeing him could not be concealed from her husband; and knowing too that the mere presence of the prince would excuse him in her

eyes and undermine all her resolve, Mme de Clèves decided
she would pretend to be unwell. The court was too distracted
to pay attention to what she did or to discover whether her
illness was real or feigned. Only her husband could know the
truth, but she was not sorry that he should know it. So she
remained at home, little considering the great change that
was about to take place: full of her own thoughts, she was
entirely free to indulge in them. Everybody was at the King's
side. M. de Clèves returned from time to time, to give her the
news. His behaviour towards her was just as it had always
been, except that, when they were alone, there was something
a little colder and less easy in it. He had not spoken again to
her of what had occurred; and she had not had the strength,
or even considered it proper to resume the discussion.

M. de Nemours, who had expected to find a few moments
when he might speak to Mme de Clèves, was most surprised
and distressed at not having even the pleasure of seeing her.
The King's condition worsened to the point where, on the
seventh day, the doctors despaired of his life. He accepted the
certainty of death with extraordinary fortitude, all the more
admirable since he was dying as the result of so unfortunate
an accident, and at the prime of life, successful, worshipped
by his people and loved by a mistress whom he, in turn,
loved to distraction. The day before he died, he ordered that
Madame, his sister, should be married without ceremony.
The Duchesse de Valentinois's state can well be imagined.
The Queen did not permit her to see the King and sent to her
for the monarch's seals and the crown jewels, which were in
her charge. The duchess asked if the King was dead, and
when told he was not, replied:

'Then no one is yet master over me, and no one can oblige
me to give up what he entrusted to my care.'

As soon as he was dead, at the Château de Tournelles, the
Duc de Ferrare, the Duc de Guise and the Duc de Nemours
conducted the Queen Mother, the King and the Queen, his
wife, to the Louvre. M. de Nemours accompanied the Queen
Mother. As they were setting out, on foot, she held back a

few steps and told the Queen, her daughter-in-law, that she should go first; but it was easy to see that there was more of resentment than of civility beneath this compliment.

Book Four

The Cardinal de Lorraine had made himself absolute master of the Queen Mother's [22] thoughts; the Vidame de Chartres had henceforth entirely lost favour with her, and his love for Mme de Martigues (as well as his love of freedom) prevented him even from appreciating the gravity of this loss. Throughout the ten days of the King's illness, the cardinal had enough time to make plans and persuade the Queen to adopt a course favourable to his designs. In this way, as soon as the King was dead, the Queen ordered the Connétable to remain at Tournelles with the body of the late King, to perform the usual ceremonies. This commission ensured that he was removed from the scene of events and deprived him of any scope for action. He sent a messenger to the King of Navarre, telling him to come with all haste, so that they might combine forces against the Guise brothers, since he could see that they were about to concentrate power in their hands. The command of the armies was given to the Duc de Guise and control of finances to the Cardinal de Lorraine. The Duchesse de Valentinois was driven from the court, and the Connétable's declared enemy, the Cardinal de Tournon, recalled, as was Chancellor Olivier, declared enemy of the Duchesse de Valentinois. In brief, the whole complexion of the court changed. The Duc de Guise put himself on a par with the princes of the blood in carrying the King's mantle during the funeral ceremony; he and his brothers were utterly in control, not only because of the cardinal's influence with the Queen, but because her opinion was that she could dismiss them if they were to cross her, while she could not dismiss the Connétable, who had the support of the princes of the blood.

When the period of mourning was over, the Connétable came to the Louvre, where he was received very coldly by the King. He hoped for a private audience, but the King called for the Guise brothers and, in front of them, advised him to rest, saying that management of the army and of the state finances had been assigned and that, when he had need of his counsel, he would summon him to his presence. The Queen Mother received him with even greater coldness than the King, and went so far as to reprimand him for telling the late King that his children did not resemble him. The King of Navarre arrived, to no better welcome. The Prince de Condé, less imperturbable than his brother, complained openly, but his complaints were to no avail: he was dismissed from court on the pretext of his going to Flanders to sign the ratification of the peace treaty. The King of Navarre was shown a forged letter from the King of Spain, accusing him of encroaching on his domains; he was led to fear for his lands; and, finally, persuaded to make plans to return to Béarn. The Queen provided him with the means of doing so by entrusting Mme Elisabeth to his charge and even obliged him to go ahead of the princess. And, in this way, there was no one remaining at court who might offset the power of the House of Guise.

Although it was irksome for M. de Clèves not to accompany Mme Elisabeth, he could have no complaint as to the rank of the person who was preferred over him. But he regretted not undertaking the task, less because of the honour that it would have brought, than because it would have removed his wife from court without there appearing to be any motive for his doing so.

A few days after the King's death, it was decided that the court would go to Reims for the coronation. As soon as the journey was mentioned, Mme de Clèves, who had been constantly at home, feigning illness, begged her husband to agree that she should not accompany the court, but instead go to Coulommiers to take the air and attend to her health. He replied that he did not want to know whether it was for reasons of health that she was prevented from making the journey, but that he consented to her wish. He agreed easily to something that he had already decided: much though he respected his wife's virtue, he realized that it was unwise to allow her to remain close to a man whom she loved.

M. de Nemours soon learned that Mme de Clèves would not accompany the court; he could not bear to leave without seeing her and, on the eve of his departure, went to her house as late in the day as propriety would allow, in order to find her alone. Fortune favoured his plans. As he entered the courtyard, he met Mme de Nevers and Mme de Martigues who were just leaving, and who told him that they had left her alone. As he went up the stairs, his emotions were so agitated that they can only be compared to those of Mme de Clèves, on being told that M. de Nemours was coming to see her. The fear that he might speak to her of his love, the apprehension that she might reply too favourably, the anxiety that the visit might cause her husband, and the anticipation of how hard it would be either to tell him these things or to conceal them from him, all presented themselves to her in an instant and plunged her into such turmoil that she decided to avoid the one thing that perhaps she desired most of all. She sent one of her ladies to M. de Nemours, who was then in the antechamber, to say that she had suddenly been taken ill and deeply regretted not being able to accept the honour of his visit. How mortified he was at not seeing Mme de Clèves, and at not seeing her because she did not wish him to see her! He set off the next morning, with no further hope of a chance meeting. He had not spoken to her since their conversation at the Dauphine's and had reason to believe that his error in speaking to the Vidame had destroyed all his hopes. In short, he left with everything that could intensify his already bitter regret.

As soon as Mme de Clèves had somewhat recovered from her agitation at the idea of the prince's visit, all her reasons for refusing him vanished. She even thought that she was wrong to have done so and, had she dared, or had it not now been too late, she would have recalled him.

On leaving her, Mme de Nevers and Mme de Martigues

went to the Dauphine's; M. de Clèves was there. The princess asked where they had been, and they replied that they had just come from Mme de Clèves's where they had spent a part of the afternoon with a large company, but left only M. de Nemours. These words, which they thought insignificant, were not so to M. de Clèves. He must have considered that M. de Nemours could find many opportunities to speak to his wife, yet the idea that he was with her, that they were alone and that he could speak to her of his love, struck him at that moment as something so unprecedented and so unbearable that he was consumed with a more violent feeling of jealousy than ever before. He could not remain at the Queen's: he returned home, not even knowing why he was returning or whether he intended to surprise M. de Nemours. As soon as he came near his house, he searched for any sign that might indicate whether the prince was still there; he felt relief at discovering he was not and pleasure in the idea that his visit must have been brief. He told himself that perhaps it was not of M. de Nemours that he should be jealous and, though he did not really doubt it, sought to doubt; but so powerful was his conviction that he did not long remain in this welcome state of uncertainty. He went directly to his wife's room and, after speaking to her for some time on trivial matters, felt compelled to ask her what she had done and whom she had seen; so she told him. When he noticed that she did not mention M. de Nemours, he asked, trembling, whether those were all she had seen, giving her the opportunity to speak the prince's name and thus avoid the pain of her duplicity. Since she had not seen him, she said nothing, and M. de Clèves resumed, in a tone of voice that betrayed how affected he was:

'And M. de Nemours?' he asked. 'Did you not see him, or have you forgotten?'

'No, I did not see him,' she answered. 'I felt unwell and I sent one of my ladies to make my excuses.'

'So you were indisposed only for him,' M. de Clèves continued. 'Since you saw everybody, why make such a distinction for M. de Nemours? Why is he different from all the rest? Why must you be afraid even to see him? Why must you let him see that you are afraid? Why do you let him know that you use the power his love gives you over him? Would you dare refuse to see him if you did not know full well that he can distinguish between your obduracy, and mere incivility? But why must you show such obduracy towards him? From a person of your sort, madame, anything is a favour, apart from indifference.'

'I did not think,' Mme de Clèves replied, 'whatever might be your suspicions regarding M. de Nemours, that you could reprimand me for not having seen him.'

'Yet I am doing so, Madame,' he answered, 'and my suspicions are well-founded. Why not see him, if he has said nothing to you? But he has spoken, madame: if his silence alone had told you of his passion, it would not have made so great an impression on you. You were unable to tell me the whole truth, you have concealed the greater part of it from me; you even regretted the little that you had confessed, and did not have the strength to continue. I am more unfortunate than I thought and I am the most unfortunate of men. You are my wife, I love you like a mistress, yet I witness your love for another man, a man who is the most charming at court: he sees you every day and knows that you love him. Ah!' he exclaimed, 'I even imagined you were overcoming your feeling for him. I must have been mad to believe it possible.'

'I do not know,' Mme de Clèves said, sadly, 'whether you were wrong to approve of my adopting such an extraordinary course as I did; but neither do I know whether I was mistaken to think that you would treat me justly.'

'Resolve your doubts, madame,' M. de Clèves replied. 'You were mistaken. What you expected of me was as impossible as what I expected of you. How could you hope that I should be reasonable? Had you forgotten that I loved you to distraction and that I was your husband? One of these things alone can drive a man to extremes, so what must both do together? Alas, what else do they do!' he continued. 'All my feelings are nothing but violence and doubts, beyond my control. I no longer consider myself worthy of you, and you no longer seem worthy of me. I adore you, I hate you, I offend you, I beg your forgiveness; I am filled with wonder and admiration for you, and with shame at these feelings. In brief, there is no longer tranquillity or reason in me. I cannot think how I have continued to live since you spoke to me at Coulommiers and since the day when you learned from Mme la Dauphine that your story was public knowledge. I cannot puzzle out by what means it emerged, nor what passed between you and M. de Nemours on this subject: you will never explain it to me and I am not asking you to do so. I ask only that you should remember that you have made me the unhappiest man in the world.'

With these words, M. de Clèves left his wife's room and set off the next day without seeing her; but he wrote her a letter imbued with sorrow, tenderness and sincerity. Her reply was so touching and so full of reassurance as to her past and future conduct that, since these assurances were founded on truth and such were her real feelings, the letter made an impression on M. de Clèves and calmed him a little; in addition to which, as M. de Nemours was going with him to join the King, his mind was put at rest by knowing that he would not be in the same place as Mme de Clèves. Whenever she spoke to her husband, the love that he showed her, his honourable conduct, the affection that she had for him and her obligations towards him, left an impression on her that weakened the idea of M. de Nemours. But it was only for a time, and soon the idea returned with still greater force and immediacy than before.

During the first days after the prince's departure, she was scarcely aware of his absence; but soon the separation seemed cruel. Since she had first loved him, not a day had passed without her fearing, or hoping, that they would meet; and she was dismayed at the thought that it was beyond the power of chance to bring them together.

She went to Coulommiers and, since she was going there,

she arranged for them to bring some large paintings that she had had copied from originals commissioned by Mme de Valentinois for her fine residence at Anet. Every outstanding event that had occurred during the King's reign was represented in these pictures. Among these was the Siege of Metz; all those who had distinguished themselves in this action were shown in a very lifelike manner. M. de Nemours was among them and this, perhaps, was what made Mme de Clèves wish to have the painting.

Mme de Martigues, who had been unable to leave with the court, promised her that she would spend a few days at Coulommiers. Sharing the Queen's favour had not made them envious or distanced them from each other; they were friends, though they did not share their feelings. Mme de Clèves knew that Mme de Martigues loved the Vidame; but Mme de Martigues did not know that Mme de Clèves loved M. de Nemours, or that she was loved by him. Her being the Vidame's niece endeared Mme de Clèves still more to Mme de Martigues; and Mme de Clèves also felt an attachment to her, as someone who was, like herself, passionately in love and in love, moreover, with the closest friend of the man who was the object of her own affections.

Mme de Martigues came to Coulommiers as she had promised, and found Mme de Clèves living a very solitary life. She had even sought how she could be entirely alone and spend the evenings in the grounds without her servants. She would go to the pavilion where M. de Nemours had overheard her and enter the chamber that opened on the garden, Her ladies and servants would stay in the other room, or in the pavilion, and come only when called. Mme de Martigues had never seen Coulommiers; she was surprised by the beauty of the place and particularly the sweetness of this pavilion; she and Mme de Clèves would spend every evening there. Free to remain alone, at night, in the loveliest spot in the world, these two young people, whose hearts were consumed by love, would talk endlessly together; and, though they did not confide in each other, took great pleasure in conversation.

Mme de Martigues would have found it hard to leave Coulommiers, except that on doing so she was going to be with the
Vidame. She left for Chambord, where the court then was.

The coronation had been solemnized at Reims by the Cardinal de Lorraine, and the rest of the summer was to be spent
at the Château de Chambord, then newly built. The Queen
showed great pleasure at seeing Mme de Martigues and, after
expressing this several times, asked news of Mme de Clèves,
and what she was doing in the country. M. de Nemours and
M. de Clèves were both then at the Queen's. Mme de Martigues, who had greatly admired Coulommiers, spoke of all
its attractions and described the pavilion in the forest at
considerable length, mentioning Mme de Clèves's pleasure in
walking there alone during a part of the night. M. de
Nemours, who knew the place well enough to follow what
Mme de Martigues was saying, thought it not impossible that
he might be able to see Mme de Clèves, without being seen
by anyone except her. He asked Mme de Martigues to enlighten him on one or two details; and M. de Clèves, who
had been watching him all the time that Mme de Martigues
was speaking, thought he understood at that moment what
was going through his mind. The prince's questions confirmed
this idea, so that he no longer doubted M. de Nemours was
planning to visit his wife. His suspicions were well-founded.
M. de Nemours was so absorbed by the plan that, after
spending all night considering how he could carry it out, the
very next morning he begged leave to depart from the King
to go to Paris, on some pretext or other.

M. de Clèves was sure he knew the purpose of this journey;
but he resolved to learn the truth of his wife's conduct once
and for all, and not to remain any longer in a state of agoniz-
ing doubt. He wanted to leave at the same time as M. de
Nemours and go himself, secretly, to learn the outcome; but
he was afraid his departure would seem odd and that M. de
Nemours, when he heard of it, would take other measures; so
he decided to confide in one of his attendants, a gentleman
whose intelligence and loyalty he could trust. He described

the situation to him. He told him of Mme de Clèves's virtuous
conduct up to that time and ordered him to leave on the
heels of M. de Nemours, to observe him closely, to see
whether he went to Coulommiers and whether he entered the
garden by night.

The gentleman, well able to perform such a task, did so as
conscientiously as could be. He followed M. de Nemours to a
village, half a league from Coulommiers, where the prince
stopped: the gentleman easily guessed that it was to await
nightfall. He thought it better not to remain there himself,
but continued through the village and entered the forest, at a
place where he thought M. de Nemours must pass; he was
not mistaken in any of his predictions. As soon as night
came, he heard footsteps and, dark though it was, soon recognized M. de Nemours. He saw him walk round the garden,
as if listening out for any sound and choosing the place
where he might most easily enter. The fence was very high,
and there was another beyond it to prevent anyone getting
in, so it was quite difficult to find a way through. However,
M. de Nemours succeeded and, as soon as he was inside the
garden, had no trouble in discovering where Mme de Clèves
was. He saw several lights in the room; all the windows were
open and, creeping along beside the fence, he drew near,
feeling an agitation and an emotion that can easily be
imagined. He hid behind one of the windows, which served
as doors, to observe what Mme de Clèves was doing. He saw
that she was alone, but saw such astonishing beauty in her
that he was scarcely able to contain himself at the sight. It
was warm and she had nothing on her head or across her
breast except her hair, unarranged and loosely tied. She was
on a divan, with a table in front of her, on which there were
several baskets full of ribbons; she was picking some out and
M. de Nemours noticed that they were the same colours as
those he had worn at the tournament. He observed that she
was knotting them about a most unusual malacca cane which
he had carried at one time, then given to his sister, from
whom Mme de Clèves had had it, without appearing to

recognize it as one that had belonged to M. de Nemours. After completing her work with the charm and sweetness that the feelings of her heart conveyed to her face, she took a torch and went over to a large table facing the painting of the Siege of Metz that contained M. de Nemours's portrait; she sat down and began to look at the picture with the intensity of meditation that only passionate love can induce.

M. de Nemours's feelings at this moment cannot be described. To see – in the depth of night, in the loveliest spot in the world – to see the person whom he adored, to see her without her knowing that she was seen, and to see her entirely occupied with matters relating to himself and to a love that she was concealing from him, is something no other lover has ever enjoyed or imagined.

The prince was so much beside himself that he remained motionless, looking at Mme de Clèves, not considering how precious time was. When he had recovered a little, he decided that he should wait to speak to her until she came into the garden; he thought that he could do this more safely, because she would be further away from her ladies; but, seeing that she was staying in the room, he made a resolve to go in. Yet when he tried to carry it out, how agitated he felt! What terror that he might annoy her! What fear of bringing about a change in that face, in which there was such tenderness, and seeing it fill with sternness and wrath!

He told himself that it had been madness, not to come and watch Mme de Clèves without being observed, but to consider revealing himself to her; he envisaged all manner of things that he had not previously foreseen. It seemed sheer folly, in his boldness, in the middle of the night, to surprise a young woman to whom he had never yet spoken his feelings. It occurred to him that he ought not to imagine she would wish to listen and that she would be justifiably angered by the danger to which he would expose her, should anything go amiss. All his courage left him, and he was many times on the point of deciding to go back without being seen. Yet, driven on by the desire of speaking to her and reassured by the encouragement given him by everything that he had seen, he took a few paces forward, but in such an agitated state that a scarf he was wearing caught in the window and made a noise. Mme de Clèves turned round and, whether because her mind was full of the prince, or because he was at a spot where the light fell sufficiently for her to distinguish him, she thought she recognized him and, without hesitating or turning towards where he was, she went out into the place where her ladies were waiting. She was so disturbed as she entered that, to hide her emotion, she was obliged to say she felt ill; she said it also to distract everyone and allow M. de Nemours time to withdraw. When she had had time to reflect, she thought that she had been mistaken and that her imagination had deceived her into thinking she had seen M. de Nemours. She knew that he was in Chambord and considered it quite improbable that he could have risked doing something so foolhardy; several times, she wanted to go back into the room and look in the garden to see if anybody was there. Perhaps she hoped as much as she feared finding M. de Nemours; but at length reason and caution prevailed over these other feelings and she considered it better to contain her doubts than to take the risk of resolving them. For a long time, she could not decide to leave a place where she thought that the prince might be close by, and it was almost daylight when she returned to the château.

M. de Nemours had stayed in the garden as long as he could see a light; he had not lost hope of seeing Mme de Clèves once more, though he was convinced she had recognized him and only gone out of the room to avoid him; but when he saw that the doors were being closed, he concluded there was nothing further to hope. He went back and took his horse, close to the place where M. de Clèves's attendant was waiting. This gentleman followed him as far as the village from which he had left on the previous evening. M. de Nemours decided to spend the whole day there, so that he might return at night to Coulommiers, to see whether Mme de Clèves would once more be cruel enough to avoid him, or not to expose herself to being observed; though he knew real joy at having found her so filled with thoughts of him, he was nonetheless mortified that she had shown so instinctive an impulse to flee from his sight.

No passionate love was ever so tender or strong as was then felt by this prince. He set off beneath the willow trees, beside a little stream that flowed behind the house where he had been hiding. He went as far away as he could, so as not to be seen or heard by anyone. He gave free rein to the transports of love and his heart was so full that he could not refrain from shedding a few tears; but these tears were not the sort that sorrow induces alone; they were mingled with the sweetness and delight that are only to be found in love.

He began to recall everything that Mme de Clèves had done since he had fallen in love with her; what sincere and modest propriety she had always shown towards him, even though she loved him. 'For she does indeed love me,' he thought, 'she loves me, that I cannot doubt; the most solemn commitment and the greatest of favours are not more certain proof than I have had. Yet I am treated with the same severity as if I were an object of hatred; I put my hope in time, but I have nothing further to expect from it; I can see that she still maintains her defences, both against me and against herself. If I were not loved, I should think how I might make myself more appealing; but she finds me so, loves me and hides it from me. So what more is there to hope for, what change in my fate? What! Am I to be loved by the most adorable woman in the world and to enjoy that overflowing of love that comes with the first certainty of being loved, only so that I may the more cruelly suffer the pain of her unkindness? Beautiful princess, let me see that you love me,' he cried, 'let me see your feelings; if I could only know them once in my life, I should accept from then on, and for ever, that you oppress me with your severity. Look at me at least with those same eyes that I saw you cast on my portrait this evening; can you have gazed at it with such tenderness, yet so cruelly flee from my person? What frightens you? Why is my love so fearsome? You love me; it is vain to disguise it; you have yourself involuntarily given me proof of the fact. I know my good fortune, let me enjoy it, cease to make me unhappy. Is it possible,' he went on, 'that I can be loved by Mme de Clèves and yet be unhappy? How lovely she was this night! How could I resist the desire to throw myself at her feet? Had I done so, I should perhaps have persuaded her not to flee, my respect would have reassured her. But perhaps she did not recognize me; I may be tormenting myself more than I need; and the sight of a man, at such an unwonted hour, terrified her.'

Throughout the day, M. de Nemours was occupied with these thoughts. He waited impatiently for nightfall and when it came he set out again for Coulommiers. M. de Clèves's attendant, who had disguised himself to escape notice, followed him to the same place as on the previous evening and saw him go into the same garden. The prince soon learned that Mme de Clèves did not want to risk his attempting to see her again: all the doors were shut. He walked around in every direction, looking for a light, but in vain.

Mme de Clèves, guessing that M. de Nemours might return, had remained in her room. She suspected that she might not always have the strength to turn away from him and did not want to put herself in danger of speaking to him in a manner so inconsistent with her conduct up to that time.

Although M. de Nemours had no hope of seeing her, he did not immediately want to leave a place where she so often went. He spent the whole night in the garden and found some consolation at least in seeing the same objects that she saw every day. The sun had risen before he thought of returning, but finally the fear of discovery obliged him to leave.

He found it impossible to go away without seeing Mme de Clèves, so he went to visit Mme de Mercoeur, who was at that time in the house that she had close to Coulommiers. She was most astonished at her brother's arrival. He invented an excuse for his journey which was plausible enough to deceive her, and eventually schemed so well that he contrived to make her suggest herself that they go to Mme de Clèves's. The proposal was carried out the same day and M. de Nemours told his sister that he would take his leave of her at Coulommiers, in order to return directly to the King. He devised this plan of leaving her at Coulommiers with the idea that she would be the first to set out; and he thought that he had discovered an infallible means of speaking to Mme de Clèves.

When they arrived, she was walking in a broad avenue running alongside the gardens. The sight of M. de Nemours perturbed her to no small degree and dispelled any remaining doubts as to whom she had seen the previous night. The confirmation of this brought a sudden feeling of anger, when she considered how bold and imprudent his action had been. The prince noticed the coldness in her expression and was hurt by it. The conversation touched on nothing of any consequence; yet he managed to display so much wit, such consideration and admiration for Mme de Clèves that, despite herself, he succeeded in dispelling part of her initial coldness towards him.

With this reassurance, he expressed himself most curious to go and see the pavilion in the forest. He mentioned it as the most pleasant spot in the world and even gave so minute a description of it that Mme de Mercoeur told him he must have been there several times to know its attractions so well.

'But I cannot think,' said Mme de Clèves, 'that M. de Nemours has ever been inside there; the place was only completed a short time ago.'

'Still, I was there only recently,' said M. de Nemours, looking at her, 'and I am not sure whether I should be relieved that you have forgotten seeing me there.'

Mme de Mercoeur, who was studying the beauty of the garden, paid no attention to what her brother was saying. Mme de Clèves blushed, lowering her eyes without looking at M. de Nemours:

'I do not remember,' she answered, 'having seen you; and if you were there, it was without my knowledge.'

'It is true, madame,' replied M. de Nemours, 'that I went without your inviting me to do so, and spent there the sweetest and cruellest moments of my life.'

Mme de Clèves understood quite well what the prince meant, but did not reply. She considered how to prevent Mme de Mercoeur from going into that room, since M. de Nemours's portrait was there and she did not want her to see it. She was so successful in this that time passed without their noticing it and Mme de Mercoeur spoke of returning home. But when Mme de Clèves realized that M. de Nemours and his sister were not leaving together, she guessed the danger that awaited her; she found herself in the same predicament as in Paris and adopted the same course. Her resolve was strengthened to no small degree by the fear that this visit would merely confirm her husband's suspicions; and, to avoid remaining alone with M. de Nemours, she told Mme de Mercoeur that she would accompany her to the edge of the forest, and gave orders for her carriage to follow. So extreme was the prince's distress at finding that Mme de Clèves continued with the same severity towards him, that he paled instantly. Mme de Mercoeur asked if he was unwell; but he looked at Mme de Clèves, without anyone noticing, and his expression told her that he was enduring no sickness other than despair. However, he had to let them go without daring to follow and, after what he had said, could not return on a second visit with his sister. Instead, he went back to Paris and left there the following day.

M. de Clèves's gentleman had been watching him throughout: he also returned to Paris and, seeing M. de Nemours set out for Chambord, took the mailcoach so that he might arrive before him and give an account of his journey. His master had been awaiting his arrival as something that would decide his whole fate.

As soon as he saw him, he guessed, from his expression and from his silence, that what he had to tell him would be unwelcome news. For some time he remained, overwhelmed with misery, unable to speak, hanging his head. At last, he motioned to him to withdraw.

'Go,' he said. 'I can see what you have to tell me, but I do not have the strength to hear it.'

'I have nothing to tell you,' the gentleman replied, 'that amounts to any definite proof. It is true M. de Nemours went to the garden in the forest on two successive nights, and that he visited Coulommiers the following day with Mme de Mercoeur.'

'That is enough,' M. de Clèves replied, 'that is enough,' again gesturing to him to retire, 'and you need enlighten me no further.'

The gentleman was obliged to abandon his master to despair. This was as terrible as has ever been seen, and few men of such great courage and such a passionate nature as M. de Clèves, have at one and the same time suffered the pain of a mistress's infidelity and the shame of being betrayed by a wife.

M. de Clèves could not withstand the prostration of grief. The same night, he was taken with a fever, with such awful consequences that, from the start, his illness appeared very grave. Mme de Clèves was informed and came at all speed. When she arrived, his condition had worsened, and she found something so icily cold in his manner towards her that she was profoundly surprised and distressed. She even felt that he was reluctant to allow her to tend him, but thought that this was perhaps an effect of his illness.

When first she was in Blois, where the court then was, M. de Nemours could not resist the joy of knowing that she was at the same place as himself. He tried to see her and went daily to M. de Clèves's house, on the excuse of enquiring for news of him; but in vain. She did not leave her husband's room and was deeply distressed at seeing him in this state. M. de Nemours was in desperation at her being so affected: he could well imagine how much this grief rekindled her affection for M. de Clèves and how dangerous a diversion this affection might be from the love in her heart. For some time, this feeling caused him mortal pain; but the gravity of M. de Clèves's illness gave him fresh cause to hope. He saw

that Mme de Clèves might perhaps be free to follow the
dictates of her heart and that he could in the future enjoy a
succession of enduring pleasures and happiness. He could not
continue to think in this way, so great was the agitation and
exultation he felt, and he put it from his mind, fearing to
lapse into too profound a despair, should his hopes come to
nothing.

Meanwhile, M. de Clèves had been almost given up by his
doctors. In one of the final days of his illness, after a most
uncomfortable night, in the morning he said that he wanted
to rest. Mme de Clèves stayed alone in his room and it
seemed to her that, far from resting, he was suffering great
agitation. She came close and knelt beside his bed, her face
bathed in tears. M. de Clèves had decided not to reveal the
extent of his bitterness against her, but her care and her
sorrow, which at times seemed genuine to him and which he
also at times considered as evidence of her hypocrisy and
treachery, caused him such conflicting and painful feelings
that he could not contain them.

'You shed plenty of tears, madame,' he said, 'for a death
which you yourself have inflicted and which cannot cause
you the pain that you feign to endure. I am no longer in any
state to upbraid you,' he continued, his voice weakened by
sickness and pain, 'but I am dying from the cruel wound that
you have given me. Did an act so extraordinary as yours, in
speaking to me in Coulommiers, need to have so little consequence? Why inform me of your passion for M. de Nemours,
if your virtue was unable to withstand it? I admit to my
shame that I loved you to the point where I was happy to be
misled; I have longed to return to the false sense of security
from which you have now driven me. Why did you not leave
me in that untroubled blindness so many husbands enjoy? I
might perhaps have remained all my life in ignorance of your
love for M. de Nemours. I shall die,' he added. 'But know
that you make death welcome to me and that, after it had
taken away the respect and the affection that I had for you,
life appalled me. What should I do with life,' he said, 'spending

it with a person whom I have loved so much and who has so cruelly deceived me, or living apart from that same person, only to end in recriminations and outbursts of a kind so contrary to my nature and to the love I felt for you? It was greater than you knew, madame; I hid most of it, for fear of importuning you or losing a part of your respect through behaviour unsuited to a husband. In short, I deserved your heart and, once more, since I could not possess it and since I can no longer desire it, I die without any regret. Farewell, madame; you will one day mourn for a man who loved you with a true and lawful passion. You will feel the sorrow that all reasonable people feel in such affairs, and realize the difference between being loved as I loved you, and being loved by those who pretend love while only seeking the honour of seducing you. But my death will leave you free,' he added, 'and you can make M. de Nemours happy, without committing any sin. What does it matter,' he went on, 'what happens when I am no more: must I be so weak as even to think of it!'

Mme de Clèves was so far from believing that her husband could suspect her that she listened to all these words without understanding and with no other notion except that she was being reprimanded because of her liking for M. de Nemours. But at length, her eyes suddenly opened, she cried:

'I – commit a sin! The very idea is unthinkable to me. The highest virtue could not have dictated any course apart from the one I have followed, and I have never done anything that I would not wish you to have seen.'

'Would you wish me,' M. de Clèves retorted, looking at her contemptuously, 'to have witnessed the nights that you spent with M. de Nemours? Oh, madame, am I speaking of you in such terms – as a woman who has spent nights with a man?'

'No, monsieur,' she replied. 'No, it is not of me that you are speaking. I have never spent either nights or any other time with M. de Nemours. He has never seen me alone, I have never endured him, or listened to him, and I will take any oath . . .'

'Do not continue,' M. de Clèves interrupted. 'False oaths or a true confession would perhaps cause me equal distress.'

Mme de Clèves could not answer, silenced by pain and tears. Eventually, with an effort:

'At least look at me, hear me,' she said. 'If it were only a matter of my own interests, I should endure this blame; but your life is at stake. Listen to me, as you love yourself: with so much truth on my side, it is impossible that I should not convince you.'

'Would to God that you could do so!' he exclaimed. 'But what can you tell me? Was M. de Nemours not in Coulommiers with his sister? And did he not spend the two previous nights with you in the garden in the woods?'

'If that is my sin,' she answered, 'I can easily prove my innocence. I do not ask you to believe me: believe all your servants who will tell you if I went into the garden in the woods the day after M. de Nemours came to Coulommiers, and whether I did not return from there on the previous evening two hours earlier than usual.'

Then she told him how she had imagined seeing somebody in the garden. She admitted that she thought it was M. de Nemours. She spoke with such assurance, and truth persuades so easily even when it is implausible, that M. de Clèves was almost convinced of her innocence.

'I do not know,' he said, 'whether I should allow myself to believe you. I feel myself so close to death that I do not wish to see anything that might make me regret losing life. You have enlightened me too late; but I shall be eternally consoled in taking with me the idea that you are worthy of the esteem I have felt for you. I beg you to give me also the consolation of thinking that you will cherish my memory and that, had it been within your power to do so, you would have felt for me what you feel for another.'

He tried to go on, but weakness prevented him. Mme de Clèves called for the doctors; they found him almost without life. Yet he languished a few days more, and died at last with admirable fortitude.

Mme de Clèves was left in such violent anguish that she almost lost her reason. The Queen solicitously came to see her and conducted her to a convent, though she did not understand where she was being taken. Her sisters-in-law brought her back to Paris even before she was in any condition to appreciate fully the extent of her grief. When she began to have enough strength to contemplate it; when she realized the husband she had lost; and when she considered that she was the cause of his death, and that it was through the love she had felt for another that she had become its cause, the disgust she conceived for herself and for M. de Nemours cannot be described.

During these first times, the prince dared show her no other consideration except that dictated by good manners. He knew Mme de Clèves well enough to think she would not welcome any too obvious attentions; but what he later discovered made it clear he would have to continue for a long time in the same course.

One of his equerries told him that M. de Clèves's attendant, who was a close friend of his, had said, in his sorrow at the loss of his master, that M. de Nemours's journey to Coulommiers had been the cause of his death. M. de Nemours was very surprised at this; but, on reflection, he guessed a part of the truth and rightly judged what Mme de Clèves's feelings would be, and how estranged she would be from him, if she thought that her husband's illness had been caused by jealousy. He decided that he should not even remind her so soon of his name, and acted accordingly, difficult though it was for him to do so.

He went to Paris and could not refrain, in spite of himself, from calling at her door to know how she was. He learned that nobody saw her and that she had even forbidden them to tell her who had come to visit. It might be that these instructions had been given precisely because of the prince, so that she would not hear speak of him. M. de Nemours was too much in love to endure life when he was so completely deprived of seeing Mme de Clèves; thus he resolved to find some means, however difficult it might seem, to escape from a situation he found so intolerable.

The princess's sorrow exceeded the bounds of reason. She could not turn her mind from her dying husband, dying because of her and with such tender feelings towards her. She continually reviewed everything that she owed him and blamed herself for not having felt passionately towards him, as if this were something that had been in her power to do. She found consolation only in the idea that she mourned him as he deserved to be mourned and that, throughout what remained of her life, she would act only as he would have wished her to act, had he lived.

She often considered how he could have known that M. de Nemours had been to Coulommiers. She did not suspect the prince of having told him, and she thought it a matter of indifference to her if he had repeated it, so much she felt cured and removed from the love she had felt for him. Yet she was deeply perturbed at the idea that he had been the cause of her husband's death, and was pained to recall M. de Clèves's fear on his deathbed that she might marry the prince; but all these sorrows were confused with what she felt at the loss of her husband, and she thought that she had no other sorrow than this.

When several months had passed, she emerged from this deep sense of mourning that had overtaken her, and lapsed into a state of sadness and melancholy. Mme de Martigues came to Paris and was assiduous in visiting her during her stay. She spoke of the court and of everything that was happening there; and, although Mme de Clèves did not appear interested, Mme de Martigues continued to entertain her with the news.

She told her about the Vidame, M. de Guise and all those others who were distinguished for their looks or their qualities.

'As for M. de Nemours,' she said, 'I do not know if politics has taken the place of gallantry in his heart, but he is much less cheerful than he used to be, and even appears to take no interest in associating with women. He often comes to Paris and I even believe he is here at this moment.'

The name of M. de Nemours took Mme de Clèves by surprise and caused her to blush. She changed the subject and Mme de Martigues did not notice that she was perturbed.

The following day, the princess, who had been looking for something fitting her present state to occupy the time, went to see a man close by who had a peculiar way of working in silks; she had the notion that she might do something of the kind. When they had been shown to her, she noticed the door of a room where she thought there were more of the same, and asked for it to be opened. The owner replied that he did not have the key and that the room was occupied by a man who came occasionally during the day to make drawings of the fine houses and gardens that could be seen from the windows.

'He is the most distinguished man in the world,' he added, 'and does not at all resemble a person reduced to earning his living. Whenever he comes here, I see him look always at the houses and gardens, but at no time do I see him work.'

Mme de Clèves listened very closely to these remarks. What Mme de Martigues had told her about M. de Nemours sometimes being in Paris connected in her imagination with this handsome man who came close to where she lived, to suggest the idea of M. de Nemours, and of M. de Nemours determined to see her, which made her vaguely uneasy, though she did not know why. She went to the windows, to see what they overlooked, and found that they surveyed the whole of her garden and the front of her apartments. And, when she was back in her room, she could easily distinguish that same window at which she had been told the man stood. The thought that it was M. de Nemours completely altered her state of mind: she was no longer in that sort of sadness and calm to which she had been growing accustomed, but felt disturbed and anxious. Finally, unable to remain indoors, she went out to take some air in a garden beyond the city limits where she thought she would be alone. When she got there, she imagined this was correct: she saw no sign of anybody and walked for quite a long while.

After going through a small wood, she noticed a kind of summerhouse open on all sides, at the end of an avenue in the remotest corner of the garden. She walked towards it, and as she drew near, saw a man lying on one of the benches, appearing deeply enwrapped in thought: she recognized him as M. de Nemours. She stopped dead at the sight of him; but her servants, who were following, made some noise which roused M. de Nemours from his reverie. Without looking to see the cause, he got up from his place, in order to avoid the people coming towards him, and turned down another path, making such a low bow that it prevented him even from seeing the objects of his salutation.

If he had known whom he was avoiding, how urgently he would have retraced his steps; but he continued along the avenue, and Mme de Clèves saw him leave by a gate behind which his carriage was waiting. How great was the effect of this fleeting vision on Mme de Clèves's heart! How great was the dormant passion that once more consumed her, and with what force! She went and sat in the place that M. de Nemours had just left, and remained there, as if stricken. The prince appeared to her more adorable than anything in the world, having loved her for so long, passionately, respectfully and loyally, rejecting everything for her, even respecting her grief, dreaming that he might see her without dreaming that he might be seen, leaving the court, which was his delight, merely to gaze on the walls that enclosed her and meditate in places where he could not hope to meet her; in short, a man worthy of being loved for his fidelity alone, and one for whom she felt so strong an attraction that she would have loved him even if he had not loved her; yet, moreover, a man of high quality, in rank equal to herself. Duty and virtue no longer stood in the way of her feelings, all obstacles had been removed and nothing remained of their former state, except M. de Nemours's passion for her and that which she felt for him.

None of these ideas had previously occurred to the princess. Her grief at the death of M. de Clèves had preoccupied her too much for her to consider them. M. de Nemours's presence brought them crowding into her mind; but, when it was entirely taken up with them and she also remembered that this same man, whom she thought of as being able to marry her, was the man whom she had loved while her husband was still alive and who was the cause of his death; that, as he died, he had even expressed his fear that she might marry him; then her stern conscience was so mortified at the notion, that she found it scarcely less of a sin to marry M. de Nemours, than she had thought it to love him during her husband's lifetime. She gave herself over to these ideas, which were so hostile to her happiness, and strengthened them further with several arguments concerning her peace of mind and the misfortunes she could anticipate, were she to marry the prince. At last, after staying for two hours in the same place, she returned home persuaded that she should avoid seeing him, since to do so would be precisely the opposite of what duty required.

But that certainty, imposed by reason and virtue, did not carry her heart. This remained attached to M. de Nemours with such force that she was reduced to a truly pitiable state, and was unable to rest: she spent one of the most unhappy nights that she had ever known. In the morning, her first impulse was to go and see if there was anyone at the window overlooking hers; she went and saw M. de Nemours. She was startled and drew back with a suddenness that made the prince think he had been recognized. Often, he had wanted to be seen, since the time when his love had discovered this means of seeing Mme de Clèves; and now, when he did not expect to have that pleasure, he went to meditate in the same garden where she had found him.

Exhausted at length by his unhappiness and uncertainty, he resolved to try some means to clarify his fate. 'What am I waiting for?' he wondered. 'I have known for a long time that she loves me; she is free and duty no longer stands in her

way. Why should I be reduced to seeing her, without being seen
or speaking to her? Can love have deprived me utterly of reason
and daring, and made me so different from what I have been in
the other passions of my life? I had to respect Mme de Clèves's
grief, but I am paying it too much respect and giving it time to
extinguish her feelings for me.'

At this point, he considered what means he should use to
see her. He thought that nothing any longer obliged him to
conceal his love for her from the Vidame de Chartres. He
decided to speak to him and declare his intentions towards
his niece.

The Vidame was then in Paris: everyone had come to the city
to order clothing and finery, before following the King who was
to accompany the Queen of Spain. So M. de Nemours went to
the Vidame and made a full admission of everything he had
hidden up to then, except for Mme de Clèves's feelings, not
wishing to appear to know them.

The Vidame received all that he told him with great joy
and assured him that, without knowing his mind, he had
often thought that, since losing her husband, Mme de Clèves
was the only woman worthy of him. M. de Nemours begged
him to arrange for him to speak to her and learn her feelings
on the matter.

The Vidame proposed accompanying him to visit her, but M.
de Nemours felt that she would be shocked by this, as she was
not yet seeing anybody. They decided that the Vidame must
invite her to his house, on some pretext or other, and that M. de
Nemours would enter by a secret staircase, so as not to be seen.
Everything happened as they had arranged: Mme de Clèves
arrived, the Vidame went to greet her and showed her into a
large study at the far end of his apartments. Shortly afterwards,
M. de Nemours came in, as if by chance. Mme de Clèves was
most astonished at seeing him; she blushed and tried to hide her
blushes. At first, the Vidame talked about other things; then he
went out, on the excuse of having some instructions to give his
servants. He told Mme de Clèves that he begged her to welcome
his guest and that he would return shortly.

It is impossible to describe the feelings of M. de Nemours and Mme de Clèves on finding themselves alone and able to speak for the first time. For some while they remained without saying anything, until at last M. de Nemours broke the silence:

'Madame, can you forgive M. de Chartres,' he said, 'for having given me an opportunity to see you and speak with you that you have always so cruelly denied me?'

'I should not forgive him,' she replied, 'for having forgotten my present circumstances and the danger to my reputation.'

On saying this, she wanted to leave; but M. de Nemours, restraining her, said:

'Fear nothing, madame. No one knows I am here and you need fear no danger. Hear me out, madame, hear me, if not through kindness to me, then at least for your own sake and to protect you from the excess to which I must surely be driven by a passion I can no longer control.'

For the first time, Mme de Clèves ceded to her feelings for M. de Nemours and, looking at him with eyes full of beauty and tenderness:

'But what can you hope to obtain,' she said, 'from the indulgence you require of me? You may well regret having obtained what I shall surely regret having granted. You deserve a happier fate than you have enjoyed up to now; a happier one, too, than you can hope to find in the future, unless you seek it elsewhere!'

'I, madame!' he said. 'Am I to seek my happiness elsewhere! Is there any for me, except to be loved by you? Though I have never declared it to you, I cannot believe, madame, that you are unaware of my love or that you do not know that none could ever be truer or more impassioned than mine. Has it not been tried in ways that you cannot know? And to what trials have you submitted it by your severity?'

'Since you wish me to speak and since I am resolved to it,' Mme de Clèves replied, sitting down, 'I shall do so with a frankness that you would be hard put to find in those of my sex. I shall not tell you that I did not observe your attachment to me; you would probably not believe me if I were to say so. Hence, I admit not only that I observed it but that I interpreted it as you would have wished me to do.'

'And if you did observe it, madame,' he interrupted, 'is it possible that you could remain unmoved? Might I dare ask if it made no impression on your heart?'

'That you must have seen from the way I behaved,' she replied. 'But I should like to know what you thought of it.'

'I could only dare speak about that if I were in a more favourable situation,' he answered. 'And what I might tell you has too little to do with the outcome. All I can say, madame, is that I should dearly have wished you had not confessed what you were hiding from me to M. de Clèves and that, what you allowed me to see, you had concealed from him.'

'How did you discover,' she asked, with a blush, 'that I had confessed something to M. de Clèves?'

'I learned it from your own lips, madame,' he replied. 'But, to excuse my boldness in listening, consider whether I misused what I had heard, whether my hopes were raised by it and whether I became bolder in speaking to you.'

He began to tell her how he had overheard her conversation with M. de Clèves, but she interrupted before he had finished.

'Tell me no more,' she said. 'I can now understand how you came to know so much. You already appeared only too well-informed at the Dauphine's, after she had learned of this matter from those in whom you confided.'

M. de Nemours then described the means by which this came about.

'Do not justify yourself,' she continued. 'I forgave you a long time ago without hearing your reasons. But since you learned from me something that I intended always to hide from you, I admit that you aroused feelings in me that I had never experienced before seeing you, and of which I even had so little conception that they took me at first by surprise, still further increasing the turmoil that always accompanies them.

I confess this with less shame at a time when it is not sinful for me to do so and when you have seen that my conduct was not governed by my feelings.'

'Madame,' said M. de Nemours, falling to his knees, 'can you imagine that I do not expire at your feet, transported with joy?'

'What I have told you,' she replied, smiling, 'is nothing more than you know already only too well.'

'Oh, madame,' he answered, 'how different it is from learning such a thing by chance, to hear it from your own lips and see that you truly wish me to know it!'

'You are right,' she said, 'I do truly wish you to know it and I do find it pleasing to tell you. I am not even sure whether I am saying it more from love of myself than of you. For in the end this admission will lead to nothing and I shall follow the strict rules that my duty commands.'

'You cannot think of such a thing, madame,' M. de Nemours replied. 'No duty binds you now, you are free. And, if I dared, I should even say that it is within your power to make it your duty, one day, to preserve the feelings you have for me.'

'My duty,' she answered, 'forbids me ever to think of anyone, and less of you than of anyone else in the world, for reasons which you do not know.'

'Perhaps I do know them, madame,' he said. 'But these are not valid reasons. I believe that M. de Clèves considered that I had been more fortunate than I was and imagined that you had sanctioned a folly to which I was driven by passion, without your consent.'

'Let us not speak of that adventure,' she said. 'I cannot bear to think about it: it fills me with shame and also with too much distress, because of its consequences. It is only too true that you were the cause of M. de Clèves's death: the suspicions that he derived from your ill-considered conduct cost him his life, no less than if you had taken it with your own hands. Consider what course I should have to follow, if the two of you had gone to such lengths and the same misfortune been the result. I know that it is not the same thing in the eyes of the world; but to mine there is no difference, since I know that it was through you and because of me that he died.'

'Ah, madame!' exclaimed M. de Nemours. 'What is this phantom of duty that you raise up in the path of my happiness? What! Must some empty and baseless fancy prevent you bestowing happiness on a man whom you do not hate? What! Have I nurtured the hope of spending my life with you; has fate induced me to love the most admirable person in the world; have I not seen in her everything proper to make her the beloved object of my affections; has she found me not detestable, and have I seen in her conduct nothing but what can make a woman desirable? For, indeed, madame, you are perhaps the only person in whom those two things have ever been seen to the degree that they are in you. Every man who marries a woman by whom he is loved, marries her in fear and trembling, when he considers her behaviour towards him in relation to other men. But with you, madame, there is nothing to fear, only to admire. Have I, as I say, conceived such immense happiness, simply to see you yourself raise up obstacles against it? Oh, madame, you forget that you have distinguished me above all other men; or, rather, you have not distinguished me, you have mistaken me, and I flattered myself.'

'You did not flatter yourself,' she replied. 'The arguments of duty would perhaps seem less compelling to me without this distinction that you doubt in yourself, and which convinced me of the misfortune of an attachment to you.'

'I have nothing to answer, madame,' he said, 'when you tell me that you fear misfortune; but I must admit that after everything you have been kind enough to say, I did not expect to hear you reason so unkindly.'

'My reasoning is so far from reflecting badly on you,' Mme de Clèves said, 'that I even find it hard to express.'

'Alas, madame,' he replied, 'how can you be afraid of too much flattering me, after what you have just said?'

'I wish to continue to speak with the same sincerity as I began,' she went on. 'And I shall do so, without all the reserve and delicacy that I should show in a first conversation. But I beg you to listen without interrupting.

'I believe that I owe your attachment for me the meagre return of hiding none of my feelings, but revealing them as they are. In all probability, this will be the only time in my life when I shall allow myself freely to exhibit them to you; yet I cannot confess, without shame, that the certainty of no longer being loved by you as I now am appears to me such a dreadful misfortune that, were the arguments of duty not insurmountable, I doubt whether I could bring myself to risk such unhappiness. I know you are free, as I am, and our situation is perhaps such that no public blame could be attached to you or to me, were we to commit ourselves to each other for ever. But does a man sustain love in such everlasting covenants? Should I hope for a miracle in my favour? And how can I prepare myself for the inevitable end of that passion, on which all my happiness would rest? M. de Clèves was perhaps the only man in the world able to preserve something of love within marriage. Fate decreed that I should be unable to profit by this good fortune; and it may also be true that his passion survived only because he found none in me. But I should not have the same means to guarantee yours: I even believe that the impediments to your love ensured its constancy. You encountered enough for you to be roused to overcome them, and my involuntary actions, or things that you learned by chance, gave you sufficient hope for you not to become disheartened.'

'Ah, madame!' interjected M. de Nemours. 'I cannot keep the silence that you require of me. You are too unjust, and show me only too clearly how little you are predisposed in my favour.'

'I admit,' she replied, 'that I may be led by passion; but it cannot blind me. Nothing can prevent me from knowing that you were born with every predisposition for courtship and every quality tending towards its success. You have already had many affairs and you will have many more; I should cease to bring you happiness; I should see you become for another what you had been for me. The pain that this would inflict would be deadly and I cannot guarantee that I should not suffer the misfortune of jealousy. I have said too much to hide the fact that you have already made me experience this: I suffered such cruel torments on the evening when the Queen gave me the letter from Mme de Thémines, supposedly addressed to you, as to instil an idea of that emotion in me which convinces me it is the greatest of ills.

'All women, through vanity or inclination, wish to seduce you. Few are insensible to your charms, and my own experience would suggest that there are none to whom you might not appeal. I should think you always in love, and loved, and I should seldom be wrong. Yet, in this situation, I should have no choice but to endure; I do not even know if I should dare to complain. A lover may be reproached; but can one reproach a husband when one has nothing to blame except that he no longer feels love? And, even if I might become used to this kind of misfortune, could I grow accustomed to seeing the image of M. de Clèves accusing you of his death, reproaching me for having loved you and married you, and making me feel the difference between his love and yours? It is impossible,' she continued, 'to overlook such powerful arguments: I must remain in my present state and adhere to my resolve never to quit it.'

'What, madame! Do you think it possible?' exclaimed M. de Nemours. 'Do you think your resolve can withstand a man who adores you and is fortunate enough to have won your favour? It is harder than you think to resist those whom we love, and by whom we are loved. You have done so thanks to a code so strict as to be almost unexampled; but this is no longer in conflict with your feelings, and I hope you will follow them, in spite of yourself.'

'I am perfectly well aware that there is nothing harder than what I intend,' Mme de Clèves answered. 'Even as I argue it, I mistrust my strength. What I feel I owe to the memory of

M. de Clèves would be weak if it were not supported by the cause of my own peace of mind, and the arguments in favour of that must be sustained by those of duty. But, though I mistrust myself, I believe I never shall conquer my scruples, and hope also never to vanquish the feelings I have for you. They will make me miserable and I shall renounce seeing you, regardless of the cost to myself. I implore you, by whatever power I have over you, not to seek the opportunity of seeing me. I am in a condition that would make a sin of everything that might be legitimate at other times, and propriety alone forbids any communication between us.'

M. de Nemours threw himself at her feet and gave way to all the varied emotions that convulsed him. Both in his words and in his tears, he exhibited the most powerful and tenderest passion that ever possessed a human heart. That of Mme de Clèves was not indifferent to it and, looking at the prince with eyes somewhat swollen with tears:

'Why should it be,' she exclaimed, 'that I must accuse you of M. de Clèves's death? Why did I not start to know you since the time when I became free, or why not before I was engaged to another? Why has fate put such an insurmountable barrier between us?'

'There is no barrier, madame,' M. de Nemours replied. 'You alone stand in the way of my happiness; you alone are subjecting yourself to a law, to which neither morality nor reason can subject you.'

'It is true,' she responded, 'that I am sacrificing much to an idea of duty that exists only in my mind. Wait and see what time may do. M. de Clèves has only recently expired, and this figure of mortality is too close for me to have any clear view of the matter. Nonetheless, be contented with having gained the love of a woman who would never have loved anything, had she not seen you; believe that my feelings for you are everlasting and will endure regardless of what I may do. Adieu,' she said. 'This conversation shames me: I permit you, and even beg you, to report it to M. le Vidame.'

With these words, she left the room, and M. de Nemours

could not hold her. She found the Vidame in the nearest chamber. She seemed so distressed that he dared not speak to her and handed her into her carriage without a word. He returned to find M. de Nemours, who was so full of joy, sorrow, amazement and admiration – in short, of all the feelings that derive from passionate love when it is full of hope and fear – that he no longer had the use of his senses. It was a long time before the Vidame could persuade him to recount what had passed between them. He did so at last; and M. de Chartres, though not himself in love, wondered no less than M. de Nemours at the virtue, spirit and worthiness of Mme de Clèves. They considered what outcome the prince might expect; and, despite the misgivings that his love inspired, he agreed with the Vidame that Mme de Clèves could not possibly abide by her present resolve. Yet they accepted that they must follow her orders lest, should people learn of his feelings towards her, she might make some statement or undertake some public commitment that she would afterwards adhere to, fearing others might believe she had loved him while her husband was still alive.

M. de Nemours decided to follow the King. The journey was one he could not easily refuse and he determined to leave without even attempting to see Mme de Clèves again from the place where he had sometimes seen her. He begged the Vidame to speak to her. How much he told him to tell her! What an infinite succession of arguments to persuade her to vanquish her scruples! In short, part of the night had already passed before M. de Nemours thought to leave him in peace.

That was something Mme de Clèves was in no state to enjoy. It was so unprecedented a thing for her to have abandoned the constraints she had imposed on herself, to have, for the first time in her life, permitted a man to tell her he loved her and to have said that she loved him, that she could no longer recognize herself. She was amazed at what she had done; she regretted; she was overjoyed: her whole heart was filled with turmoil and passion. Once more, she examined the arguments of duty that stood in the way of her happiness;

she was distressed to find them so powerful and regretted having so persuasively shown them to M. de Nemours. Though the idea of marrying him had come to her mind the moment she saw him again in the garden, it had not impressed her with the same force as the conversation they had just had; and there were moments when she was hard put to understand how she could be miserable if they were to marry. She would greatly have wished to tell herself she was unfounded both in her scruples about the past and her misgivings for the future. Yet, at other moments, reason and duty demonstrated entirely the opposite and quickly drove her to resolve that she would never remarry and never see M. de Nemours. But this was a most painful decision to fix in a heart so deeply smitten as hers and so recently abandoned to the charms of love. At length, to find some repose, she thought that it was not yet essential to suffer the agony of taking any decision; propriety gave her a considerable space of time to make up her mind; but she did resolve to hold fast and to have no communication with M. de Nemours.

The Vidame came to see her and served the prince, arguing his cause with all possible intelligence and devotion; but he could not change her mind as to her conduct, or that which she had imposed on M. de Nemours. She told him that her plan was to remain in her present state; that she knew this was difficult to carry out; but that she hoped to have the strength to do it. She so persuaded him of her attachment to the idea that M. de Nemours had been the cause of her husband's death, and how strongly she believed that marrying him would be contrary to her duty, that the Vidame feared it might be unwise to remove this idea. He did not tell the prince what he thought but, in his account of the conversation, left him with all the hope that a man who is loved must reasonably feel.

The next day, they left and joined the King. The Vidame wrote to Mme de Clèves, at M. de Nemours's request, about the prince; and in a second letter closely following the first, M. de Nemours added a few lines in his own hand. But Mme de Clèves, not wishing to infringe upon the rules she had set for herself and fearing the accidents that can happen with letters, instructed the Vidame that she would not accept any from him, if he continued to mention M. de Nemours; and her request was so emphatic that the prince himself begged him not to mention his name again.

The court accompanied the Queen of Spain as far as Poitou. While they were away, Mme de Clèves kept to herself and, the further she was removed from M. de Nemours and everything that might call him to mind, the more she thought of M. de Clèves, whose memory she made it a point of honour to preserve. Her reasons for not marrying M. de Nemours seemed strong as far as duty was concerned and insurmountable for her peace of mind. The end of the prince's love and the evils of jealousy, which she felt were inseparable from marriage, pointed to the certain misery towards which she was heading; but she saw too that she was undertaking an impossible task in trying to resist in the presence of the most delightful man in the world, whom she loved and who loved her, and to resist him on grounds that were contrary neither to morality nor to propriety. She considered that absence alone and distance could give her some strength; she thought that she needed them both to maintain her resolve not to enter an engagement, and even to prevent her from seeing M. de Nemours; and she decided to take a fairly long journey, to pass all the time that convention dictated she should live in seclusion. Some estates she owned in the Pyrenees seemed the most appropriate place to choose. She left a few days before the return of the court; and, before leaving, wrote to the Vidame to beg him not to think of seeking news of her, or writing to her.

M. de Nemours suffered as much from this journey as another might at his mistress's death. He felt real pain at the thought of not seeing Mme de Clèves for so long and this, above all, at a time when he had experienced the pleasure of seeing her and seeing her moved by his love. Yet he could do nothing except bewail his fate, much though his suffering was increased. Mme de Clèves, whose mind had endured such turmoil, became desperately ill as soon as she arrived at her estates, and news of this reached the court. M. de Nemours was inconsolable: in his anguish, he gave way to despair and folly. The Vidame was hard put to prevent him from exhibiting his feelings in public, and also to contain him and dissuade him from going in person to discover how she was. M. le Vidame's relationship with the princess and his friendship provided an excuse for sending many couriers. At length, they were told she was out of immediate danger; but she still languished in a wasting sickness that left little hope for her life.

So long and so near a contemplation of death showed Mme de Clèves the things of this life in a much different light from the one in which we see them in health. The inevitability of dying, which she felt to approach, accustomed her to become detached from everything, and the length of her illness made this a habit. However, when she recovered from this condition, she found that M. de Nemours was not effaced from her heart; but she summoned to her help, in protecting herself against him, all the arguments she could find for never marrying him. A considerable conflict took place in her. Finally, she overcame the remains of her passion, already weakened from the feelings inspired by her illness. The idea of death had returned her to thinking of M. de Clèves, and his memory, which was in harmony with her duty, became deeply impressed on her heart. The passions and relationships of this world appeared to her as they do to those who can take a broader and more distant view of them. Her health was much weakened and this helped her to preserve these feelings; but, knowing what circumstances can do to the wisest resolve, she had no wish to risk undermining her own, or to return to the places where the object of her former love resided. She retired, on the pretext of a change of air, to a convent, without declaring any fixed resolve to abandon court life.

When M. de Nemours first heard of it, he realized the

significance of this retreat and how great it was. At that moment, he felt he had no further hope; but the loss of his hopes did not prevent him from employing every means to bring Mme de Clèves back. He got the Queen to write, he got the Vidame to write, he got him to go; but all was in vain. The Vidame saw her: she did not tell him that she had taken any decision. Yet he believed that she would never return. Finally, M. de Nemours went in person, on the pretext of taking the waters. She was extremely surprised and upset to learn of his arrival. She sent word to him, through a person of worth who was dear to her and whom she had with her at that time, that she begged him not to find it untoward if she did not expose herself to the danger of seeing him and so destroy, by his presence, feelings which she ought to preserve; that she would like him to know that, having found her duty and peace of mind in conflict with the inclination she had felt to belong to him, the other things of this world must appear so indifferent to her that she renounced them for all time; that she no longer thought of anything except the other life, and that she had no further desire except to see him in the same frame of mind as herself.

M. de Nemours thought he would die of sorrow in the presence of the woman who brought him this message. He begged her twenty times to go back to Mme de Clèves and contrive for him to see her; but the woman told him that Mme de Clèves had not only forbidden her to bring any message from him, but even to report their conversation. So, at last, the prince had to depart, as overwhelmed with grief as any man can be when he has lost all hope of seeing again a person whom he loves with the strongest, most natural and most legitimate passion that has ever been. Yet he was still not finally discouraged, and did all that might persuade her to alter her mind. At length, when many years had passed, time and absence assuaged his pain and extinguished his feelings. Mme de Clèves lived in a manner suggesting that she would never relent. For a part of the year she stayed in the convent, and the remainder at home; but in seclusion and in holier occupations than those of the strictest religious order; and her life, which was somewhat brief, left inimitable examples of virtuous conduct.

Notes

BOOK ONE

1 ... *the last years of the reign of Henri II* ... *Diane de Poitiers, Duchesse de Valentinois* (p. 23): Mme de Lafayette situates the events of the novel towards the end of the Valois dynasty, which started in 1328 with the accession of Philippe VI. Henri II, son of François I (1494–1547), born in 1519, succeeded his father in 1547 and reigned until his death in 1559. While still Duc d'Orléans, he fell in love with Diane de Poitiers (1499–1566), the wife of Louis de Brézé: though the future King was barely in his teens and she was twenty years his senior, she remained his mistress for the rest of his life. The King's elder brother, François de Valois, died at Tournon, aged nineteen, in 1536. Three years before that, Henri had married Catherine de Médicis (1519–89), daughter of Lorenzo de' Medici, whose three sons were to become the last Valois Kings, as François II (reigned 1559–60), Charles IX (reigned 1560–74) and Henri III (reigned 1574–89), the dynasty being succeeded by that of the Bourbons, which survived until the abolition of the monarchy in 1792.

Mme de Lafayette's main sources for the history of the period were: François de Mézeray's *Abrégé de l'histoire de France*, published in 1643–51; Pierre de Brantôme's anecdotal memoirs, *Recueil d'aucuns discours*, written in the second half of the sixteenth century (though not published until a few years before *La Princesse de Clèves*); Michel de Castelnau's *Mémoires*, also written in the late sixteenth century and published with additions by Jean Le Laboureur in 1659 under the title *Additions aux Mémoires de Castelnau*; Pierre Matthieu's *Histoire de France* (1631); and various works, including André du Chesne's *Histoire d'Angleterre* (1614), the translations of Francis Godwin's *Annals* (1647) and Nicholas Sanders' account of the English Reformation, *De Origine ac Progressu Schismatis Anglicani*, for the stories of Mary Stuart and Anne Boleyn. She follows these sources very closely for descriptions of events and characters.

2 *Mme Elisabeth de France ... Mary Stuart ... Madame* (p. 24): Elisabeth, Henri II's daughter, married Philip II of Spain in June 1559, at the age of fourteen, and died in 1568. It was believed in France that Don Carlos, Philip's son, had fallen in love with her and that the Spanish King had her poisoned (which explains the remark about her beauty proving fatal). Mary Stuart (1542–87), later Queen of Scots, was the daughter of James V of Scotland and Marie de Guise. In 1558, the year when the novel begins, she married François II, heir to the throne, or Dauphin, and as the Dauphine, or Reine Dauphine, she plays a leading role in the story. 'Madame', the King's sister, is Marguerite de France (1525–74) who, after her marriage to the Duc de Savoie in July 1559, became Marguerite de Savoie. She was a poet and patronized other writers, including the poet Ronsard.

3 *The King of Navarre ... the Duc de Guise ... the Cardinal de Lorraine ... the Chevalier de Guise ... the Prince de Condé* (pp. 24–5): The King of Navarre (1518–62), is Antoine de Bourbon, whose son became the first King of the Bourbon dynasty as Henri IV in 1559. The Guise brothers – François I (1519–63), Duc de Guise, Charles (1524–74), Cardinal de Lorraine, and François (1534–63), Chevalier de Guise and Grand Prieur – whose influence and ambition are emphasized throughout the novel, were the three sons of Claude, Duc de Lorraine, created Duc de Guise in 1527. When Henri II was succeeded in 1559 by the fifteen-year-old François II, then in 1560 by the nine-year-old Charles IX, the Guise family became the most powerful in France. François I, the eldest brother, had distinguished himself particularly by recapturing Calais from the English, and his son Henri (1550–88) took part in the Saint-Bartholomew's Day massacre of Huguenots in 1572. The Prince de Condé, Louis de Bourbon (1530–69), a leader of the Protestant faction in the Religious Wars, was assassinated after being taken prisoner at the Battle of Jarnac, in 1569.

Mme de Lafayette's description of the brilliance of Henri II's court in its last two years – the period of the novel – and of the still friendly rivalry between these nobles implies an awareness that this was founded on a fragile balance, and that it was soon to give way to bitter sectarian conflicts: in this way, the historical and political background to the story harmonizes with its sense of the need for order in human relationships and of the impermanence of human happiness.

4 *The Duc de Nevers . . . the Prince de Clèves . . . the Vidame de Chartres . . . the Duc de Nemours* (p. 25): With the last three, Mme de Lafayette comes to the central male characters in the novel. François de Clèves (1516–62), Duc de Nevers, had three sons, the second, Jacques, being the Prince de Clèves in question. For the purposes of the story, the author tampers with the historical record: in reality, Jacques married Diane de la Marck and died at the age of twenty, in 1564, after a life of ill-health. His early death and his obscurity make him a plausible figure to lend his name to the hero of the novel. 'Vidame' was a feudal title, originally applied to the person who acted on behalf of a bishop in certain secular matters. The Vidame de Chartres was François de Vendôme, Prince de Chabanois (1524–62), the uncle of the fictitious heroine (Mlle de Chartres, then Mme de Clèves), and the main confidant of the hero, the Duc de Nemours. Jacques de Savoie, Duc de Nemours, is also a historical figure: born in 1531, he married the Duc de Guise's widow, Anne d'Este, in 1566. Mme de Lafayette takes much of her description of him from Brantôme (see Note 1), together with the details of the interest shown in him, as a possible consort, by Queen Elizabeth I (though she brings the negotiations forward by a year or two).

5 *The Connétable de Montmorency . . . the Maréchal de Saint-André* (p. 26): The Connétable was supreme commander of the army. In the text of the novel, I have left this title in French, instead of finding an English equivalent ('constable' does not quite convey the dignity of the office). Anne, Duc de Montmorency (1492–1567), fell out of favour under François I after being suspected of treason. As mentioned in the next paragraph, his son François married an illegitimate daughter of Henri II. Jacques d'Albon, Maréchal de Saint-André, was to die in battle in 1562. He appears here as a leading figure in the court who was not attached to any faction, while the competition between the Connétable and the Guise family suggests its underlying instability.

6 *. . . a succession of victories* (p. 27): The struggle between France and the Holy Roman Empire, under Charles V, continued into Henri II's reign. The Battle of Saint-Quentin, in 1557, was a disaster for the French army under Montmorency, who had defeated the forces of the Empire at Renti three years earlier. The Duc de Guise successfully defended Metz in 1552

and won Calais in 1558. Peace negotiations were opened at Cercamp in October 1558.

7 *The Queen of Navarre* (p. 34): Jeanne d'Albret (1528–72), daughter of Henri, King of Navarre, married Antoine de Bourbon in 1548, and he succeeded to the title (see Note 3).

8 ... *the marriages of younger brothers* (p. 35): The marriage settlement of a younger brother would divide the family wealth.

9 *Chastelart* (p. 36): Pierre de Boscasel de Chastelart (1540–64). His tragic love for Mary Stuart is celebrated (and the subject of a poem by Swinburne): he was executed after being found hiding in her room.

10 ... *the death of his father ... occurred around the same time* (p. 38): The Duc de Nevers did not die until 1562, but Mme de Lafayette disposes of him here to leave the Prince de Clèves free to marry.

11 ... *(though I do not know by what means)* (p. 46): Mme de Lafayette, however, knows perfectly well by what means, but decides that delicacy should prevent Mme de Chartres from spelling it out: Brantôme, with hardly less delicacy, says that Diane, aged fourteen, sacrificed 'her most precious possession' to the King.

12 *The seventeen provinces* (p. 48): The Spanish Netherlands.

13 *The Cardinal de Tournon and the Amiral d'Annebauld* (p. 49): Tournon (1497–1562) was a leading political figure under François I; Annebauld, or Annebault (d. 1552), was appointed admiral in 1543. Mme de Lafayette's sources mention their banishment, as well as that of Villeroy and Taix (in the following paragraph), but not that of Chancellor Olivier, who seems to have held on to his post. The story of Brissac also comes from Mézeray's *Abrégé de l'histoire de France* (see Note 1).

BOOK TWO

14 ... *the princess* (p. 73): Elisabeth de France, who married Philip II in June 1559. See Note 2.

15 ... *a man ... who had a great reputation for astrology* (p. 77): Luc Gauric. The story is taken from Le Laboureur (see Note 1). Nostradamus is also supposed to have predicted the King's death.

16 *Mme Marguerite, Duchesse d'Alençon* (p. 80): Marguerite d'Angoulême (1492–1549), sister of François I, married first the Duc d'Alençon and, after his death, Henri d'Albret, King of Navarre. Her daughter Jeanne, from this second marriage, was the mother of the future King Henri IV (see Note 7). Marguerite was the author of the *Heptaméron*, a collection of stories modelled on Boccaccio's *Decameron*. They were edited in 1558.

Mme de Lafayette draws on various sources for the story of Anne Boleyn and Henry VIII, notably André du Chesne, Le Laboureur and Sanders (see Note 1).

17 *It was published* ... (p. 85): The following paragraph is taken almost word for word from a document reproduced in Pierre Matthieu's history of the period (see Note 1) and, though Mme de Lafayette has omitted some technicalities, the intention is to provide local colour, so I have not annotated the jousting terms.

18 ... *to take Rhodes* (p. 88): From the Turks, who had captured it from the Knights Hospitaliers in 1523. The Chevalier de Guise died in 1563.

19 *The Queen* (p. 94): Catherine de Médicis. Le Laboureur (see Note 1) mentions the rumours of her relationship with the Vidame.

BOOK THREE

20 *The Amboise conspiracy* (p. 109): A Huguenot plot in 1560, directed against the Guise brothers.

21 *The Duc d'Albe* (p. 122): The duke was to act as proxy for Philip II. Mme de Lafayette's description of the marriage ceremony is taken from a book by Père Anselme, *Le palais de la gloire*, published in 1663, and her account of the tournament comes mainly from Brantôme (see Note 1). As usual, she follows her sources quite closely.

BOOK FOUR

22 *The Queen Mother* (p. 139): Catherine de Médicis, later also referred to as 'the Queen'. Following the King's accidental death, the Guise brothers are able to establish their ascendancy with her help, and the balance between the different factions at court is

destroyed, leaving the way open for the religious and political strife of the next three decades. After this summary of events, the narrative makes virtually no further reference to politics.

In Book One, Mme de Chartres warned her daughter not to judge court life by appearances ('what appears to be the case hardly ever is'). Henri II's authority managed to contain conflicts of ideology and ambition, but this 'ordered turbulence' could not survive his death ('the complexion of the court changed'), and the dismissal of the Guise brothers' enemies is open and brutal. There is a parallel here with Mme de Clèves's breach of social convention (however admirable her motives) in telling her husband of her feelings for the Duc de Nemours, as well as her obsession with avoiding any circumstances that might allow Nemours to make an open declaration of his love to her. The implication is that harmonious relations between states, political factions and individuals are governed by conventions, one of which is that certain things are better left unsaid.

FOR THE BEST IN PAPERBACKS, LOOK FOR THE

In every corner of the world, on every subject under the sun, Penguin represents quality and variety – the very best in publishing today.

For complete information about books available from Penguin – including Puffins, Penguin Classics and Arkana – and how to order them, write to us at the appropriate address below. Please note that for copyright reasons the selection of books varies from country to country.

In the United Kingdom: Please write to *Dept E.P., Penguin Books Ltd, Harmondsworth, Middlesex, UB7 0DA.*

If you have any difficulty in obtaining a title, please send your order with the correct money, plus ten per cent for postage and packaging, to *PO Box No 11, West Drayton, Middlesex*

In the United States: Please write to *Dept BA, Penguin, 299 Murray Hill Parkway, East Rutherford, New Jersey 07073*

In Canada: Please write to *Penguin Books Canada Ltd, 2801 John Street, Markham, Ontario L3R 1B4*

In Australia: Please write to the *Marketing Department, Penguin Books Australia Ltd, P.O. Box 257, Ringwood, Victoria 3134*

In New Zealand: Please write to the *Marketing Department, Penguin Books (NZ) Ltd, Private Bag, Takapuna, Auckland 9*

In India: Please write to *Penguin Overseas Ltd, 706 Eros Apartments, 56 Nehru Place, New Delhi, 110019*

In the Netherlands: Please write to *Penguin Books Netherlands B.V., Postbus 3507, 1001 AH, Amsterdam*

In West Germany: Please write to *Penguin Books Ltd, Friedrichstrasse 10–12, D–6000 Frankfurt/Main 1*

In Spain: Please write to *Alhambra Longman S.A., Fernandez de la Hoz 9, E–28010 Madrid*

In Italy: Please write to *Penguin Italia s.r.l., Via Como 4, I-20096 Pioltello (Milano)*

In France: Please write to *Penguin Books Ltd, 39 Rue de Montmorency, F-75003 Paris*

In Japan: Please write to *Longman Penguin Japan Co Ltd, Yamaguchi Building, 2–12–9 Kanda Jimbocho, Chiyoda-Ku, Tokyo 101*

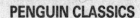